W9-AVR-157

He couldn't bear the thought that McCall might be in danger.

Restless, he picked up his cell phone again when he heard a vehicle coming up the road.

Luke shaded his eyes as he watched the cloud of dust draw closer. Definitely a pickup.

Squinting into the sun, he saw the sheriff's department logo on the side and couldn't believe his eyes.

McCall?

He watched her drive into his yard, hoping this was a social visit, knowing it probably wasn't. Had something happened and she was here to give him the bad news?

He stood in the shade as she climbed out of her pickup. Her dark hair shined in the fading sunlight. She moved with long-legged grace toward him. And as always, he was hit with such a need for this woman that it almost dropped him to his knees.

Turning back to his work, he drove a nail into another two-by-four, warning himself not to get his hopes up, that her being here had nothing to do with him. Or that kiss last night.

B.J. DANIELS

GUN-SHY BRIDE

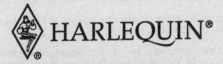

HARLEQUIN®

TORONTO • NEW YORK • LONDON
AMSTERDAM • PARIS • SYDNEY • HAMBURG
STOCKHOLM • ATHENS • TOKYO • MILAN • MADRID
PRAGUE • WARSAW • BUDAPEST • AUCKLAND

If you purchased this book without a cover you should be aware that this book is stolen property. It was reported as "unsold and destroyed" to the publisher, and neither the author nor the publisher has received any payment for this "stripped book."

From the beginning my husband, Parker, has been there for me. He was the one who encouraged me to quit my paying job even though he knew how hard it would be for us financially. He's always believed in me and takes up the slack so I can just write. He's my hero. This book, which may be my all time favorite, is for him.

Recycling programs for this product may not exist in your area.

ISBN-13: 978-0-373-69465-5

GUN-SHY BRIDE

Copyright © 2010 by Barbara Heinlein

All rights reserved. Except for use in any review, the reproduction or utilization of this work in whole or in part in any form by any electronic, mechanical or other means, now known or hereafter invented, including xerography, photocopying and recording, or in any information storage or retrieval system, is forbidden without the written permission of the publisher, Harlequin Enterprises Limited, 225 Duncan Mill Road, Don Mills, Ontario, Canada M3B 3K9.

This is a work of fiction. Names, characters, places and incidents are either the product of the author's imagination or are used fictitiously, and any resemblance to actual persons, living or dead, business establishments, events or locales is entirely coincidental.

This edition published by arrangement with Harlequin Books S.A.

For questions and comments about the quality of this book please contact us at Customer_eCare@Harlequin.ca.

® and TM are trademarks of the publisher. Trademarks indicated with ® are registered in the United States Patent and Trademark Office, the Canadian Trade Marks Office and in other countries.

www.eHarlequin.com

Printed in U.S.A.

ABOUT THE AUTHOR

B.J. Daniels wrote her first book after a career as an award-winning newspaper journalist and author of thirty-seven published short stories. That first book, *Odd Man Out*, received a four-and-a-half-star review from *RT Book Reviews* and went on to be nominated for Best Intrigue for that year. Since then she has won numerous awards including a career achievement award for romantic suspense and many nominations and awards for best book.

Daniels lives in Montana with her husband, Parker, and two springer spaniels, Spot and Jem. When she isn't writing, she snowboards, camps, boats and plays tennis. Daniels is a member of Mystery Writers of America, Sisters in Crime, International Thriller Writers, Kiss of Death and Romance Writers of America.

To contact her, write to B.J. Daniels, P.O. Box 1173, Malta, MT 59538 or e-mail her at bjdaniels@mtintouch.net. Check out her Web page at www.bjdaniels.com.

Books by B.J. Daniels

CAST OF CHARACTERS

Luke Crawford—The game warden was after a poaching ring—and the woman he'd lost ten years before.

McCall Winchester—The deputy sheriff had been running from the past until she discovered the grave and her life changed.

Ruby Bates Winchester—The waitress and mother had a secret she'd kept from her daughter all these years.

Trace Winchester—He'd disappeared twenty-seven years ago, leaving behind a pregnant wife and a lot of speculation about where he'd gone.

Pepper Winchester—The matriarch of the family had been a recluse for the past twenty-seven years.

Enid Hoagland—The disagreeable gatekeeper at Winchester Ranch. It was her job to keep everyone away from the lady of the house.

Buzz Crawford—The former game warden didn't seem to be enjoying his retirement. Or was guilt bothering him?

Eugene Crawford—He'd been like a brother to his cousin Luke—just like Cain was one to Abel.

Sheriff Grant Sheridan and his wife, Sandy—The two seemed to have no secrets from each other. Or did they?

Red Harper—The secret that had been eating away at him for the past twenty-seven years was finally about to come out.

Chapter One

The wind howled down the ravine as Deputy Sheriff McCall Winchester poked what appeared to be a mud clod with the toe of her cowboy boot.

The thunderstorm last night had been a gully-washer. As her boot toe dislodged some of the mud, she saw that the pile of objects in the bottom of the gully was neither mud nor rock.

"Didn't I tell you?"

McCall looked up at the man standing a few feet away. Rocky Harrison was a local who collected, what else? Rocks.

"It's always better after a rainstorm," he'd told her when he'd called the sheriff's department and caught her just about to go off duty after working the night shift.

"Washes away the dirt, leaves the larger stones on top," Rocky had said. "I've found arrowheads sitting on little columns of dirt, just as pretty as you please and agates large as your fist where they've been unearthed by a good rainstorm."

Only on this bright, clear, cold spring morning, Rocky had found more than he'd bargained for.

"Human, ain't they," Rocky said, nodding to what he'd dug out of the mud and left lying on a flat rock.

"You've got a good eye," McCall said as she pulled out her camera, took a couple of shots of the bones he'd found. They lay in the mud at the bottom of the ravine where the downpour had left them.

With her camera, McCall shot the path the mud slide had taken down from the top of the high ridge. Then she started making the steep muddy climb up the ravine.

As she topped the ridge, she stopped to catch her breath. The wind was stronger up here. She pushed her cowboy hat down hard, but the wind still whipped her long dark hair as she stared at the spot where the rain had dislodged the earth at the edge. In this shallow grave was where the bones had once been buried.

Squinting at the sun, she looked to the east. A deep, rugged ravine separated this high ridge from the next. Across that ravine, she could make out a cluster of log buildings that almost resembled an old fort. The Winchester Ranch. The sprawling place sat nestled against the foothills, flanked by tall cottonwood trees and appearing like an oasis in the middle of the desert. She'd only seen the place from a distance from the time she was a child. She'd never seen it from this angle before.

"You thinking what I am?" Rocky asked, joining her on the ridge.

She doubted that.

"Somebody was buried up here," Rocky said. "Probably a homesteader. They buried their dead in the backyard, and since there is little wood around these parts, they didn't even mark the graves with crosses, usually just a few rocks laid on top."

McCall had heard stories of grave sites being disturbed all over the county when a road was cut through or even a basement was dug. The land they now stood on was owned by the Bureau of Land Management, but it could have been private years ago.

Just like the Winchester land beyond the ravine which was heavily posted with orange paint and signs warning that trespassers would be prosecuted.

"There's a bunch of outlaws that got themselves buried in these parts. Could be one of them," Rocky said, his imagination working overtime.

This less-civilized part of Montana had been a hideout for outlaws back in the late 1890s or even early 1900s. But these remains hadn't been in the ground that long.

She took a photograph of where the body had been buried, then found herself looking again toward the Winchester Ranch. The sun caught on one of the large windows on the second floor of the massive lodge-style structure.

"The old gal?" Rocky said, following her gaze. "She's your grandmother, right?"

McCall thought about denying it. After all, Pepper Winchester denied her very existence. McCall had never even laid eyes on her grandmother. But then few people had in the past twenty-seven years.

"I reckon we're related," McCall said. "According to my mother, Trace Winchester was my father." He'd run off before McCall was born.

Rocky had the good sense to look embarrassed. "Didn't mean to bring up nothin' about your father."

Speaking of outlaws, McCall thought. She'd spent her life living down her family history. She was used to it.

"Interesting view of the ranch," Rocky said, and reached into his pack to offer a pair of small binoculars.

Reluctantly, she took them and focused on the main house. It was much larger than she'd thought, three stories with at least two wings. The logs had darkened from the years, most of the windows on at least one of the wings boarded up.

The place looked abandoned. Or worse, deteriorating from the inside out. It gave her the creeps just thinking about her grandmother shutting herself up in there.

McCall started as she saw a dark figure appear at one of the second floor windows that hadn't been boarded over. Her grandmother?

The image was gone in a blink.

McCall felt the chill of the April wind that swept across the rolling prairie as she quickly lowered the binoculars and handed them back to Rocky.

The day was clear, the sky blue and cloudless, but the air had a bite to it. April in this part of Montana was unpredictable. One day it could be in the seventies, the next in the thirties and snowing.

"I best get busy and box up these bones," she said, suddenly anxious to get moving. She'd been about to go off shift when she'd gotten Rocky's call. Unable to locate the sheriff and the deputy who worked the shift after hers, she'd had little choice but to take the call.

"If you don't need my help…" Rocky shifted his backpack, the small shovel strapped to it clinking on the canteen he carried at his hip as he headed toward his pickup.

Overhead a hawk circled on a column of air and for

a moment, McCall stopped to watch it. Turning her back to the ranch in the distance, she looked south. Just the hint of spring could be seen in the open land stretching to the rugged horizon broken only by the outline of the Little Rockies.

Piles of snow still melted in the shade of the deep ravines gouged out as the land dropped to the river in what was known as the Missouri River Breaks. This part of Montana was wild, remote country that a person either loved or left.

McCall had lived her whole life here in the shadow of the Little Rockies and the darker shadow of the Winchester family.

As she started to step around the grave washed out by last night's rainstorm, the sun caught on something stuck in the mud.

She knelt down to get a better look and saw the corner of a piece of orange plastic sticking out of the earth where the bones had been buried.

McCall started to reach for it, but stopped herself long enough to swing up the camera and take two photographs, one a close-up, one of the grave with the corner of the plastic visible.

Using a small stick, she dug the plastic packet from the mud and, with a start, saw that it was a cover given out by stores to protect hunting and fishing licenses.

McCall glanced at Rocky's retreating back, then carefully worked the hunting license out enough to see a name.

Trace Winchester.

Her breath caught in her throat but still she must have made a sound.

"You say somethin'?" Rocky called back.

McCall shook her head, pocketing the license with her father's name on it. "No, just finishing up here."

Chapter Two

Inside her patrol pickup, McCall radioed the sheriff's department. "Looks like Rocky was right about the bones being human," she told the sheriff when he came on the line.

"Bring them in and we'll send them over to Missoula to the crime lab. Since you're supposed to be off shift, it can wait till tomorrow if you want. Don't worry about it."

Sheriff Grant Sheridan sounded distracted, but then he had been that way for some time now.

McCall wondered idly what was going on with him. Grant, who was a contemporary of her mother's, had taken over the job as sheriff in Whitehorse County after the former sheriff, Carter Jackson, resigned to ranch with his wife Eve Bailey Jackson.

McCall felt the muddy plastic in her jacket pocket. "Sheriff, I—" But she realized he'd already disconnected. She cursed herself for not just telling him up front about the hunting license.

What was she doing?

Withholding evidence.

She waited until Rocky left before she got the small

shovel and her other supplies from behind her seat and walked back over to the grave. The wind howled around her like a live animal as she dug in the mud that had once been what she now believed was her father's grave, taking photographs of each discovery and bagging the evidence.

She found a scrap of denim fabric attached to metal buttons, a few snaps like those from a Western shirt and a piece of leather that had once been a belt.

Her heart leaped as she overturned something in the mud that caught in the sunlight. Reaching down, she picked it up and cleaned off the mud. A belt buckle.

Not just any belt buckle she saw as she rubbed her fingers over the cold surface to expose the letters. *W I N C H E S T E R.*

The commemorative belt buckle was like a million others. It proved nothing.

Except that when McCall closed her eyes, she saw her father in the only photograph she had of him. He stood next to his 1983 brand-new black Chevy pickup, his Stetson shoved back to expose his handsome face, one thumb hooked in a pocket of his jeans, the other holding his rifle, the one her mother said had belonged to his grandfather. In the photo, the sun glinted off his commemorative Winchester rifle belt buckle.

She opened her eyes and, picking up the shovel, began to dig again, but found nothing more. No wallet. No keys. No boots.

The larger missing item was his pickup, the one in the photograph. The one he allegedly left town in. Had he been up here hunting? She could only assume so, since according to her mother, the last time she saw

Trace was the morning of opening day of antelope season—and his twentieth birthday.

Along with the hunting license, she'd found an unused antelope tag.

But if he'd been hunting, then where was his rifle, the one her mother said he had taken the last time she saw him?

McCall knew none of this proved absolutely that the bones were her father's. No, that would require DNA results from the state crime lab, which would take weeks if not months.

She stared at the grave. If she was right, her father hadn't left town. He'd been buried on the edge of this ridge for the past twenty-seven years.

The question was who had buried him here?

Someone who'd covered up Trace Winchester's death and let them all believe he'd left town.

Her hands were shaking as she boxed up the bones and other evidence—all except the license still in her coat pocket—and hiked back to her rig. Once behind the wheel, she pulled out the plastic case and eased out the license and antelope tag.

The words were surprisingly clear after almost thirty years of being buried in the mud since the plastic had protected the practically indestructible paper.

Name: Trace Winchester. Age: 19. Eyes: dark brown. Hair: Black. Height: 6 ft 3 inches. Weight: 185.

He'd listed his address as the Winchester Ranch, which meant when he'd bought this license he hadn't eloped with her mother yet or moved into the trailer on the edge of Whitehorse.

There was little information on the license, but McCall had even less. Not surprising, her mother, Ruby

Bates Winchester, never liked talking about the husband who'd deserted her.

Most of what McCall had learned about her father had come from the rumors that circulated around the small Western town of Whitehorse. Those had portrayed Trace Winchester as handsome, arrogant and spoiled rotten. A man who'd abandoned his young wife, leaving her broke and pregnant, never to be seen again.

According to rumors, there were two possible reasons for his desertion. Trace had been caught poaching—not his first time—and was facing jail. The second was that he'd wanted to escape marriage and fatherhood since McCall was born just weeks later.

A coward *and* a criminal. Trace solidified his legacy when he had left behind a young, pregnant, heartbroken wife and a daughter who'd never been accepted as a Winchester.

As McCall stood on that lonely windblown ridge, for the first time she realized it was possible that everyone had been wrong about her father.

If she was right, Trace Winchester hadn't run off and left them. He'd been buried under a pile of dirt at the top of this ridge for the past twenty-seven years—and would have still been there if it hadn't been for a wild spring storm.

NORTH OF WHITEHORSE, Luke Crawford pulled down a narrow, muddy road through the tall, leafless cottonwoods along the Milk River. The only other tracks were from another pickup that had come down this road right after last night's rainstorm.

The road ended at the edge of a rancher's wheat field,

the same rancher who'd called saying he'd heard gunshots just before daylight.

Luke parked next to the fresh truck tracks. Past the tall old cottonwoods, down the slow-moving river, he could make out a small cabin tucked in the trees.

Just the sight of McCall Winchester's home stirred up all the old feelings. Luke cursed himself that he couldn't let go, never had been able to. Now that he was back in town as the new game warden, there was no way they weren't going to cross paths.

He could just imagine how that would sit with McCall.

Over the years, he'd followed her career with the sheriff's department and had heard she'd bought a place on the river. He'd also heard that she seldom dated and as far as anyone knew there was no man in her life.

That shouldn't have made him as relieved as it did.

He noticed now that her sheriff's department pickup wasn't parked next to the cabin. Had she worked the night shift last night or the early-morning one?

With a curse, he realized she might have heard the shots the rancher had reported or seen someone coming up the river road. He had no choice but to stop by and ask her, he told himself.

He sure as hell wasn't going to avoid her when it appeared there was a poaching ring operating in the river bottom. This was the second call he'd gotten in two weeks.

The thought of seeing her again came with a rush of mixed emotions and did nothing to improve his morning. He could just imagine the kind of reception he'd get, given their past. But now that he was back, there would be no avoiding each other—not in a town the size of Whitehorse.

Luke swore and got out, telling himself he had more to worry about than McCall Winchester as he saw the bloody drag trail in the mud. Taking his gear, he followed it.

RUBY WINCHESTER HAD JUST finished with the lunch crowd when McCall came into the Whitehorse Diner.

McCall felt light-headed after the morning she'd had. She'd come back into town, boxed up the bones and the other evidence, along with a request to compare the DNA of the bones with that of the DNA sample she'd taken from swabbing the inside of her mouth.

Even though the sheriff had told her to wait until her shift tomorrow, she'd mailed off the package to the crime lab without telling anyone. She was now shaking inside, shocked by what she'd done. Withholding evidence was one thing. Requesting the DNA test without proper clearance was another. She was more than jeopardizing her job.

But she couldn't wait months to know the truth. She'd bought herself some time before the report came back, and she knew exactly how she was going to use it.

"You want somethin' to eat?" her mother asked as McCall took one of the stools at the counter. "I could get you the special. It's tuna casserole. I'm sure there's some left."

McCall shook her head. "I'm good."

Ruby leaned her hip against the counter, eyeing her daughter. "Somethin' wrong?"

McCall glanced around the small empty café. Ruby hadn't cleaned off all of the tables yet. The café smelled like a school cafeteria.

"I've been thinking about my father. You've never really told me much about him."

Ruby let out a snort. "You already know about him."

"All you've ever told me is that he left. What was he like?" And the real question, who would want to kill him?

"What's brought this on?" Ruby asked irritably.

"I'm curious about him. What's wrong with that? He was my father, right?"

Ruby narrowed her gaze. "Trace Winchester *was* your father, no matter what anyone says, okay? But do we have to do this now? I'm dead on my feet."

"Mom, you're always dead on your feet, and you're the only one I can ask."

Ruby sighed, then checked to make sure Leo, the cook, wasn't watching before reaching under the counter to drag out an ashtray. She furtively lit a cigarette from the pack hidden in her pocket.

McCall watched her take a long drag, blow out smoke, then wave a hand to dissipate the smoke as she glanced back toward the kitchen again.

According to Montana law, Ruby wasn't supposed to be smoking in the café, but then laws and rules had never been something Ruby gave a damn about.

She picked nervously at the cigarette, still stalling.

"It's a simple enough question, Mom."

"Don't get on your high horse with me," Ruby snapped.

"I want to know about my father. Why is that so tough?"

Ruby met her gaze, her eyes shiny. "Because the bastard ran out on us and because I—" Her voice broke. "I never loved anyone the way I loved Trace."

That surprised her, since there'd been a string of

men woven through their lives as far back as McCall could remember.

Ruby bit her lip and looked away. "Trace broke my heart, all right? And you know damned well that his mother knows where he is. She's been giving him money all these years, keeping him away from here, away from me and you."

"You don't know that," McCall said.

"I know," Ruby said, getting worked up as she always did when she talked about Pepper Winchester. "That old witch had a coronary when she found out Trace and I had eloped."

More than likely Pepper Winchester had been upset when she'd heard that her nineteen-year-old son had gotten Ruby pregnant. McCall said as much.

"You're her own flesh and blood. What kind of grandmother rejects her own granddaughter? You tell me that," Ruby demanded.

"Was my father in any trouble other than for poaching? I've always heard that Game Warden Buzz Crawford was after him for something he did the day before he disappeared," McCall said, hoping to get her mother off the subject of Pepper Winchester.

Ruby finished her cigarette, stubbing it out angrily and then cleaning the ashtray before hiding it again under the counter. "Your father didn't leave because of that stupid poaching charge."

"Why do you say that?"

"Trace had gotten off on all the other tickets Buzz had written him. He wasn't afraid of Buzz Crawford. In fact…"

"In fact?"

Ruby looked away. "Everyone in town knew that Buzz was gunning for your father. But Trace said he wasn't worried. He said he knew something about Buzz...."

"Blackmail?" McCall uttered. Something like that could get a man killed.

LUKE CRAWFORD FOLLOWED the drag trail through the thick cottonwoods. Back in here, the soft earth hadn't dried yet. The wind groaned in the branches and weak rays of sunlight sliced down through them.

The air smelled damp from last night's storm, the muddy ground making tracking easier, even without the bloody trail to follow.

It was chilly and dark deep in the trees and underbrush, the dampness making the April day seem colder. Patches of snow had turned to ice crystals on the shady side of fallen trees and along the north side of the riverbank.

Luke hadn't gone far when he found the kill site. He stopped and squatted down, the familiar smell of death filling his nostrils. The gut pile was still fresh, not even glazed over yet. A fine layer of hair from the hide carpeted the ground.

Using science to help him if he found the poachers, he took a DNA sample. Poachers had been relatively safe in the past if they could get the meat wrapped and in the freezer and the carcass dumped in the woods somewhere.

Now though, if Luke found the alleged poacher, he could compare any meat found in a freezer and tell through DNA if it was the same illegally killed animal.

In the meantime, he'd be looking for a pickup with mud on it and trying to match the tire tracks to the vehicle the poachers had been driving.

Pushing himself to his feet, Luke considered who might be behind the poaching. It generally wasn't a hungry Whitehorse family desperate enough to kill a doe out of season. In this part of Montana, ranchers donated beef to needy families, and most families preferred beef over venison.

Nor did Luke believe the shooters were teenagers out killing game for fun. They usually took potshots from across the hood of their pickups at something with antlers after a night of boozing—and left the meat to rot.

As he followed the drag trail to where the poacher had loaded the doe into the back of his truck, he studied the tire tracks, then set about making a plaster cast.

While it dried he considered the footprints in the soft mud where the poachers' truck had been parked. Two men.

After taking photos and updating his log book, he packed up, and glancing once more toward McCall's cabin, went to give the rancher his assessment of the situation before filing his report.

Luke knew his chances of catching the poachers were slim. Not that his Uncle Buzz would have seen it that way. Buzz Crawford had built a reputation on being the toughest game warden Montana had ever seen.

But Luke tended to write more warnings than tickets and knew he couldn't solve every crime in the huge area he covered. He didn't have the "kill gene," as his uncle often told him, and that explained the problem between him and Buzz.

The problem between him and McCall Winchester, his first love—hell, the only woman he'd ever truly loved—was a whole lot more complicated.

McCALL WAS STILL CONSIDERING the ramifications of her father possibly blackmailing the former game warden. "If Trace had something on Buzz—"

"I don't know that for sure," Ruby hedged. "Your father really didn't need to blackmail anyone. His mother and the Winchester money would have gotten him out of any trouble he got into."

Not this kind of trouble, McCall thought.

But she knew what her mother was getting at. White-horse was a small town and deals were made between local judges and some families. McCall also knew the legendary Buzz Crawford. He wouldn't have taken well to blackmail.

"So if my father wasn't worried about this poaching charge…" And apparently he hadn't been, if he'd gone hunting the next morning on that ridge. "Then why did you think he ran off?"

Ruby waved a hand through the air. "I was pregnant and crazy with hormones, out of my mind half the time, and Trace…"

"You fought a lot," McCall guessed after having seen how her mother's other relationships had gone over the years. "Did you have a fight the morning before he… disappeared?"

Ruby looked away. "Why do you we have to talk about this? Trace and I were both young and hotheaded. We fought, we made up." She shrugged. "There was no one like Trace." She smiled as if lost for a moment in the past.

And for that moment, Ruby looked like the pregnant young woman in love that she'd been in the few photographs McCall had of her—usually in uniform, alone, at the café.

The moment passed. Ruby frowned. "No matter what you've heard, Trace didn't leave because of you."

"So did he take anything when he left—clothes, belongings?"

"Just his pickup and his rifle. He would have made a good father and husband if his mother had stayed out of it. Pepper Winchester has a fortune, but she wouldn't give him a dime unless he got out of the marriage to me and made me say my baby was someone else's. What kind of mother puts that kind of pressure on her son?"

McCall didn't want her mother to take off on Pepper Winchester again. Nor was she ready to tell her mother what she'd found up on the ravine south of town without conclusive evidence.

She got to her feet. "I need to get going."

"You sure you don't want some tuna casserole? I could get Leo to dish you up some for later. You have to eat and it's just going to get thrown out."

"Naw, thanks anyway." She hugged her mother, surprised how frail Ruby was and feeling guilty for upsetting her. "I didn't mean to bring up bad memories."

"All that was a long time ago. I survived it."

"Still, I know it wasn't easy." McCall could imagine how hurt her mother must have been, how humiliated in front of the whole town, that her husband had left her pregnant, broke and alone. McCall knew how it was to have the whole town talking about you.

"It wasn't so bad," Ruby said with a smile. "Within a couple of weeks, I had you."

McCall smiled, feeling tears burn her eyes as she left,

her hand in her pocket holding tight to the hunting license—the only definite thing she had of her father's—unless she counted his bad genes.

WORD ABOUT THE BONES FOUND south of town had traveled the speed of a wildfire through Whitehorse. McCall heard several versions of the story when she stopped for gas.

Apparently most everyone thought the bones were a good hundred years old and belonged to some outlaw or ancestor.

By the time McCall left Whitehorse, the sun and wind had dried the muddy unpaved roads to the southeast. The gumbo, as the locals called the mud, made the roads often impassible.

McCall headed south into no-man's-land on one of the few roads into the Missouri Breaks. Yesterday she'd driven down Highway 191 south to meet Rocky. But there were no roads from the ridge where she'd stood looking across the deep gorge to the Winchester Ranch.

Getting to the isolated ranch meant taking back roads that seldom saw traffic and driving through miles and miles of empty rolling wild prairie.

Over the years McCall had thought about just showing up at her grandmother's door. But she'd heard enough horror stories from her mother—and others in town—that she'd never gotten up the courage.

The truth was, she didn't have the heart to drive all the way out there and have her grandmother slam the door in her face.

Today though, she told herself she was on official

business. Of course one call to the sheriff would blow that story and leave her in even more hot water with her boss.

But already in over her head, McCall felt she'd been left little choice. Once the report came back from the crime lab—and she gave up the hunting license—it would become a murder investigation and she would be not only pulled off the case, but also locked out of any information the department gathered because of her personal connection to the deceased.

Before that happened, she hoped to get the answers she so desperately needed about her father—and who had killed him.

She knew it would be no easy task, finding out the truth after all these years. Her mother was little help. As for the Winchesters, well, she'd never met any of them. Trace had been the youngest child of Call and Pepper Winchester.

His siblings and their children had all left the ranch after Trace disappeared and had never returned as far as McCall knew. Her grandmother had gone into seclusion.

The Winchester Ranch had always been off-limits for McCall—a place she wasn't welcome and had no real connection with other than sharing the same last name.

The fact that her father had been buried within sight of the ranch gave her pause, though, as McCall slowed to turn under the carved wooden Winchester Ranch arch.

In the distance she could see where the land broke and began to fall as the Missouri River carved its way through the south end of the county. Nothing was more isolated or wild than the Breaks and the Winchester Ranch sat on the edge of this untamed country.

It gave her an eerie feeling just thinking of her grandmother out here on the ranch, alone except for the two elderly caretakers, Enid and Alfred Hoagland. Why had Pepper closed herself off from the rest of her family after Trace disappeared? Wouldn't a mother be thankful she had other children?

McCall drove slowly down the ranch road, suddenly afraid. She was taking a huge chance coming out here. Even if she wasn't shot for a trespasser, she knew she would probably be run off without ever seeing her grandmother.

Weeds had grown between the two tracks of the narrow, hardly used road. Enid and Alfred only came into Whitehorse for supplies once a month, but other than that were never seen around. Nor, McCall had heard, did Pepper have visitors.

As she drove toward the massive log structure, she was treated to a different view of the ranch from that on the ridge across the ravine.

The lodge had been built back in the 1940s, designed after the famous Old Faithful Lodge in Yellowstone Park. According to the stories McCall had heard, her grandfather Call Winchester had amassed a fortune, tripling the size of his parents' place.

There had always been rumors around Whitehorse about Call Winchester—the man McCall has been named for. Some said he made his fortune in gold mining. Others in crime.

The truth had remained a mystery—just like the man himself. Call had gone out for a horseback ride one day long before McCall was born, and as the story goes, his horse returned without him. His body was never to be found. Just like his youngest son, Trace. Until now.

An old gray-muzzled heeler with one brown and one blue eye hobbled out to growl beside McCall's patrol pickup.

She turned off the engine, waiting as she watched the front door of the lodge. The place looked even larger up close. How many wings were there?

When no one appeared, she eased open her vehicle door, forcing the dog back as she stepped out. The heeler stumbled away from her still growling. She kept an eye on him as she walked to the front door.

She didn't see any vehicles, but there was an old log building nearby that looked as if it was a garage, large enough to hold at least three rigs.

While she'd never seen her grandmother, McCall had run across Pepper's housekeeper, Enid—an ancient, broomstick-thin, brittle woman with an unpleasant face and an even worse disposition.

McCall had heard a variety of stories about Enid Hoagland, none of them complimentary. The house-keeper and her husband apparently took care of Pepper. Enid did the cooking and cleaning. Her husband, Alfred, did upkeep on the isolated ranch.

Some said the Hoaglands acted as guards to protect and care for Pepper. Others were of the opinion that the old couple kept Pepper Winchester hostage on the ranch to make sure they got the Winchester fortune when she died instead of her heirs.

McCall knocked at the weathered door, glancing around as she waited. A quiet hung over the wind-scoured place as if everything here had withered up and died.

She knocked harder and thought she heard a sound on the other side of the door. "Sheriff's Department. Open up."

After a long moment, the door creaked slowly open. An old woman appeared on the other side, and for a moment McCall thought she was about to come face-to-face with her grandmother.

But as the light flowed into the dark entry, she saw that it was only Enid Hoagland.

Enid scowled at her. "What do you want?" she demanded by way of greeting.

"I need to speak with Pepper Winchester."

"That isn't possible. Mrs. Winchester doesn't see anyone." She started to close the door, but McCall stuck a booted foot in the doorway.

"I'm sorry, but she'll have to see me unless you want me to come back with a warrant to search the house," McCall bluffed. "Tell her it's Deputy Sheriff McCall Winchester."

A malicious light flickered on in Enid's close-set gray eyes. "You're making a mistake," she said under her breath.

McCall feared the old woman was right.

A sound like the tinkling of a small bell came from deep in the lodge. Enid seemed to hesitate. "You will regret this."

McCall didn't doubt it. The older woman stepped aside and the deputy sheriff entered her father's family home for the first time in her life.

Chapter Three

Enid led McCall into what could only be called a parlor. The decor was old-time Western, the rustic furnishings dated as if the house had been sealed for more than thirty years.

McCall was too nervous to sit. She'd forced her way in here, and now she wasn't sure what she would say to her grandmother when she finally saw her for the first time.

At the sound of faint footfalls in the hallway, she turned, bracing herself, and yet she was still shocked. Nothing could have prepared her for the elderly woman who stepped into the room.

Pepper Winchester was surprisingly spry for seventy-two. She stood, her back ramrod straight, her head angled as if she was irritated. Her face was lined but there was something youthful about her. She was tall and slim, elegant in her black silk caftan.

Her hair, which had apparently once been dark like McCall's, was now peppered with gray. It trailed down her slim back in a single loose braid. Her eyes were ebony, her cheekbones high, just like McCall's.

The resemblance was both striking and shocking. McCall had had no idea just how much she looked like her grandmother.

If Pepper Winchester noticed the resemblance, her demeanor gave no notice of it. Nor was there any indication that she knew who McCall was.

"Yes?" she demanded.

McCall found her voice. "I'm Deputy Sheriff McCall Winchester."

Had the dark eyes widened just a little?

"I need to ask you a few questions."

"I'm sure my housekeeper told you I don't see visitors."

But you saw me. Why was that? Not because of the threat of a warrant. "I wouldn't have bothered you if it wasn't important. It's about your son Trace's disappearance."

"Have you found him?" The hope in her grandmother's voice and posture was excruciating. So was the fear she heard there. And yet, Pepper Winchester had to know that if there was any news of Trace, the sheriff would have been here—not some lowly deputy.

"I'm investigating his disappearance," McCall said quickly, taking out her notebook and pen.

"After twenty-seven years?" Pepper asked in disbelief. She seemed to shrink, all the starch coming out of her, all the spirit. "What's the point?"

"When was the last time you saw your son?"

Pepper shook her head, her dark eyes dimming in the dull light. "I should think you would know that, since I gave that information to the sheriff at the time."

McCall saw that this had been a mistake. What had she hoped to accomplish? She had wanted to see her grandmother. And now she had. The best thing she could do was to leave before Pepper Winchester got on the phone to the sheriff.

But she'd come too far. She couldn't leave things like this. Nor had she gotten what she'd come for. "Is there anyone who might have wanted to harm him?"

Pepper raised her head slightly, her dark eyes locking with McCall's. "Other than your mother?"

"Did your son have any enemies?"

"No." Instantly, she corrected herself. "Buzz Crawford. He hated my family, Trace in particular." Her voice broke as she said her son's name.

Again the former game warden's name had come up in relation to Trace.

"Was your son blackmailing Buzz Crawford?"

"*What?* Who would even say something like that? Your *mother?*" She raised her nose into the air. "My son didn't have to resort to blackmail. He was a *Winchester*. He wasn't going to serve any jail time. I would have seen to that."

Her grandmother's gaze flicked over her, anger and impatience firing those dark eyes, then she sighed deeply and started to walk away, signaling this conversation was over.

"Then why did you think he left town? Because you cut him off financially?" McCall asked, unable to hold back. "Or because you were demanding he divorce my mother and renounce the child she was carrying?"

Pepper Winchester spun back around, eyes narrowing dangerously. "You know nothing about my relationship with my youngest son. *Nothing*." She held up her hand before McCall could say another word. "You should leave. *Now*." With that her grandmother turned and disappeared through the door.

McCall closed her notebook and looked up to find Enid Hoagland framed in the doorway, a smug little smile on the horrid woman's face.

"You are not to ever disturb Mrs. Winchester again," Enid said as she walked McCall to the door and closed it firmly behind her.

Standing on the front step, McCall took a deep breath of the crisp spring air. Her heart seemed to struggle with each beat. What had she been thinking coming out here to see the grandmother who had denied her all these years? Still denied her.

Letting out the breath, McCall walked to her pickup, her eyes burning. She could feel someone watching her, the gaze boring into her back. Her grandmother? Or that awful Enid?

She slid behind the wheel, anxious to get away before she shed the tears now blurring her eyes. She wouldn't give either old woman the satisfaction of seeing how much that had hurt.

PEPPER WINCHESTER STOOD at the window trembling with rage as she watched McCall drive away.

"You should have told me how much she resembles me," she said, knowing Enid was behind her even though she hadn't heard the woman approach. Trace used to say that Enid moved as silently as a ghost—or a cat burglar.

"What would have been the point?" Enid asked. "You didn't have to see her. Now you're upset and—"

Pepper spun around to face her ancient housekeeper

as the patrol pickup disappeared down the road. "Of course I'm upset. Why would she come here and ask about Trace?"

"Because she believes he was her father."

Pepper scoffed at that, just as she had when Trace told her that he'd gotten that tramp Ruby Bates pregnant. But the proof had been standing in her house just moments before.

There was no denying that McCall was a Winchester—and her father's daughter.

"You're the one who let her in," Enid complained. "I could have gotten rid of her."

When Pepper had seen the sheriff's department vehicle pull in, she'd thought it might be news about Trace and had been unable to smother that tiny ember of hope that caught fire inside her.

"She'll be back, you know," Enid warned in obvious disapproval. "She wants more than what she got this time."

Yes, Pepper suspected McCall would be back. She'd seen herself and Trace in the young brazen woman.

"So," Enid said with a sigh. "Can I get you anything?"

My son Trace. That was the only thing she wanted.

"I just want to be alone." Pepper turned back to the window, looking down at the long curve of the road into the ranch.

All this time, she'd expected a call or a visit from the sheriff. Word from someone about her son. And after twenty-seven years to have his daughter show up at her door…

Why would McCall be investigating her father's disappearance *now?* Or had that just been an excuse to come out to the ranch?

For weeks after Trace left, Pepper would stare at that road waiting for him to come down it. How many times had she imagined him driving up that road in his new black pickup, getting out, his jacket thrown over one shoulder, cowboy hat cocked back to expose his handsome face, his long jean-clad legs closing the distance as if he couldn't wait to get home.

She'd been so sure he would contact her. Eventually he would call for money. He'd known she could make his hunting violation charge go away—just as she had the others.

For that reason, she'd never understood why he would run away. She'd blamed that tramp he'd foolishly married. Trace wasn't ready for marriage, let alone a child. Especially one Pepper had been convinced would turn out to be someone else's bastard. She'd despised Ruby for trapping her son and giving Trace no way out but to leave town.

But after weeks, then months had gone by with no word, Pepper feared *she* was the reason her son had left and never came back. The thought had turned her heart to stone.

She'd walled herself up here in the lodge unable to face life outside the ranch. Worse, she'd replayed her last argument with Trace over and over in her head.

McCall was right. She *had* threatened to cut him off without a cent if he didn't divorce Ruby and denounce that bastard child she was carrying. Trace had pleaded with her to give Ruby a chance, swearing the baby was his.

Pepper sighed. Apparently, he'd been right about that at least, she thought now. She was still trembling from finally coming face-to-face with Trace's daughter. McCall.

That bitch Ruby had named the girl after her grandfather, Call Winchester, just to throw it in Pepper's face.

But there was no doubt. The girl definitely was of Winchester blood.

She frowned as she remembered something McCall had said. *"Then why did you think he'd left town?"*

McCall hadn't come to the ranch out of simple curiosity. If that were true, she would have shown up sooner.

Pepper stepped to the phone. For years, she hadn't spoken to another soul other than Enid and her housekeeper's husband, Alfred—and fortunately neither of them had much to say.

Then McCall had shown up, she thought with a curse as she dialed the sheriff's department.

LUKE SPENT A COUPLE OF HOURS looking around Whitehorse for the poachers' pickup before he headed south. His jurisdiction included everything from the Canadian border to the Missouri River—an area about the size of the state of Massachusetts.

For that reason, he put close to twenty-five thousand miles on his three-quarter-ton pickup every year. His truck was his office as well as his main source of transportation unless he was in one of the two boats he used to patrol the area's waterways.

This time of year, because of paddlefish season, he spent most of his time on the Missouri River south of Whitehorse. Today he was checking tags and watching for fishing violations. Fishing was picking up all over his area from the Milk River to reservoirs Nelson and Fort Peck.

For the next few months, he'd be spending fourteen-to fifteen-hour days watching fishermen, checking licenses and boats for safety equipment.

That wouldn't leave much time to catch the deer poachers, but he figured they knew that.

Tired from getting up at dawn, Luke headed back toward Whitehorse a little earlier than usual. His place was just to the south, his parents' old homestead that he'd bought when he'd recently returned to Whitehorse. The homestead had been sold following his parents' deaths but he'd managed to get it back.

He liked to think it was a sign that he'd made the right decision by coming back here. A sign that there was a chance for him and McCall. He was building a new house on the property and was anxious for a couple of days off to work on it.

As he drove over the rise on the road, the stark skeleton of his new house set against the sunset, he slowed. The truck parked down by his stock pond didn't look familiar.

He pulled his pickup to a stop and got out, scanning the old windbreak of Russian olive trees as he did. The unfamiliar truck had local plates. As he walked past the pickup, he saw an older outboard lying in the back in a pool of oil and the broken tip of a fishing pole floating next to it.

"Hey!"

The greeting startled him even as he recognized the voice.

His cousin Eugene Crawford stepped from behind one of the outbuildings where he'd obviously gone to take a leak. He had a fishing pole in one hand and a beer in the other.

"Grab your rod," Eugene said. "Let's catch a few."

The last thing Luke wanted to do right now was fish. He needed some shut-eye. Hopefully the poachers would take a night off and let him get some rest.

"Sorry, but I've got to hit the hay," he told his cousin.

"At least come down and watch me catch a couple."

After Luke's parents were killed in a small plane crash when he was seven, his Uncle Buzz had taken him in and he and Eugene were raised like brothers.

His cousin, who was two years older, had always looked out for him, fighting his battles, covering his back. In high school, Eugene had been the popular one, a former high school football star and a charmer with the girls.

Now Eugene lived in the past, high school being his glory days after an injury his freshman year in college ruined any chance he had to play pro football.

Since then, Eugene had struggled, going from one job to the next, having his share of run-ins with the law as well as women. Just recently divorced for the third time, Eugene seemed to be down on his luck, if that old beat-to-hell pickup he was driving was any indication.

"All right. But just for a few minutes," Luke said, giving in the way he always had when it came to Eugene.

"So, catch any poachers lately?" his cousin asked as he cast out into the pond and sat down on the edge of the earthen dam. It was an inside joke, something Buzz had always asked from the time Luke had become a game warden.

"A few," he answered, just as he always did with Buzz.

Eugene laughed as he watched his red-and-white bobber float on the dark surface of the water. Long shadows lay across the pond, the sky behind him ablaze with the setting sun.

Luke suspected his cousin hadn't just come out here to fish.

"Sit down," Eugene said, an edge to his voice. "You look like any minute you're going to check my fishing license."

It would be just like his cousin not to have one. Eugene liked to push the limits.

"I told you. I've got to get some sleep," Luke said, realizing he wasn't up to dealing with Eugene's problems right now, or his excuses.

"Sure. I know. You have a job," Eugene said sarcastically.

"Whatever it is, I'm really not up to it tonight."

"Yeah, you got your own problems, huh. Don't want to hear about mine." His cousin swore, reeled his line in, checked the bait and threw it back out. "I need money. I'm not screwing with you. It's a matter of life and death."

Luke sighed. "How much are we talking?"

"Fifty grand."

He let out a low whistle. "How the hell did you—"

"You're starting to sound like Buzz," Eugene said in a warning tone.

"Sorry, but that's a lot of money."

"You think I don't know that? I just made a few bad bets down in Billings and now they're threatening to kill me."

It was Luke's turn to swear. "How long are they giving you to come up with the money?"

"Six weeks, but that was two months ago," Eugene said. "I've heard they're looking for me."

"I don't have that kind of money." Luke had invested most everything he had in the house and land.

"You could put this place up. It's got to be worth a bunch. How many acres do you have here, anyway?"

Luke felt as if he'd been sucker punched. He waited until his initial anger had passed. "I can't do that," he said, turning to leave. He wasn't stupid enough that he didn't know what would happen if he put up his place for the money. "There are already two mortgages on it."

"Even ten thou would help," Eugene said, pleading. He didn't seem to notice the tip of his rod bend as a fish took the bait.

The fish was the only one taking the bait today. "Sorry." This was one mess Eugene would have to get out of on his own.

"Yeah, sure you're sorry," Eugene said bitterly.

Luke's cell phone rang. He checked it and groaned inwardly. "I have to take this."

"Don't let me stop you."

Luke hated leaving things this way between them. He wished there was something more he could say. But the only thing Eugene wanted to hear was that Luke was going to bail him out, just as he had done too many times in the past.

Instead, as he left he pointed to his cousin's pole. "You have a fish."

McCALL WAS ON THE OUTSKIRTS of Whitehorse when she got the call on her cell phone. The moment she heard the sheriff's voice, she knew.

"Where are you?" Grant asked.

"On the edge of town. Something up?" She hadn't

heard anything on her radio. There was little crime in Whitehorse. The weekly sheriff's reports consisted of barking dogs, checks on elderly residents, calls about teens making too much noise and a few drunk and disorderlies.

The sheriff seemed to hesitate. "Pepper Winchester phoned me."

McCall had been waiting for the other shoe to drop. Still, it hit with a thud that set off her pulse. Hadn't she known this would happen? And yet, she'd hoped blood really was thicker than water.

"Pepper seemed to think you were on sheriff's department business, investigating her son's disappearance," Grant said. "I assured her that wasn't the case. I can understand how you might have wanted to see her."

McCall said nothing, hating the pity she heard in his voice. He thought the only reason she'd gone out there was to see her grandmother.

He cleared his throat. "She said if you came back she'd have you arrested for trespassing. I'm sorry."

McCall bit back an unladylike retort. Her grandmother was turning out to be everything she'd heard she was, and the sheriff's sympathy wasn't helping.

"It might be a good idea to stay away from the Winchester Ranch," Grant said before he hung up.

As she pulled into Whitehorse, McCall's two-way radio squawked. She listened for a moment as the dispatcher said there'd been a call about a disturbance at the Mint Bar.

She started to let the other deputy on duty pick it up since she was off the clock.

But when she heard who was involved, she said she'd take the call and swung into a parking space outside the Mint.

She heard Rocky's voice the moment she opened the bar door. A small crowd had gathered around the rock collector. As she walked in, she recognized most of the men. One in particular made her regret she'd taken the call.

Rocky was at the center of the trouble but in the mix was Eugene Crawford. At a glance, she saw that both men were drunk. Eugene as usual looked as if he was itching for a fight.

"Excuse me," she said, easing her way into the circle of men around Rocky. Closing her hand around Rocky's upper arm, she said, "It's time to go home."

"Well, look who it is," Eugene said. "It's the girl deputy."

Eugene had been the school bully and she'd been his target. It was bad enough in grade school, but in high school it had gotten worse after she turned him down for a date.

"If you gentlemen will excuse us," McCall said, drawing Rocky away from the fracas.

"What's this about some grave Rocky found south of town?" Crawford demanded.

"Probably just a fish story like the one you told when you came in," one of the men ribbed Eugene.

McCall led Rocky toward the door. He was being the perfect docile drunk. A few more feet and they would be out of the bar.

"I asked you a question, *Deputy*," Eugene said, coming up behind her and grabbing her arm.

"Let go," she said as he tightened his grip on her. "Let go now, Eugene." He smelled of fish and sweat and meanness.

"Or what? You going to arrest me?" His nails bit into her flesh. "Try it," he said and gave her a shove, slamming her into the jukebox.

She staggered but didn't fall. "Going to need some backup," McCall said into her radio as Rocky leaped to her defense.

Before she could stop him, Eugene coldcocked Rocky, who hit the floor hard. Eugene was turning to take on the others who'd jumped in when the bartender came over the bar with his baseball bat.

It took McCall, Deputy Nick Giovanni and the bartender to get Eugene Crawford restrained and into handcuffs. Nick took Eugene to the jail while McCall drove Rocky home. He was quiet most of the ride.

"Are you sure you're all right?" she asked as she walked him to his front door. "I'd feel better if I took you by the emergency room at the hospital."

"I'm fine," Rocky said, looking sheepish. "I guess I have a glass jaw, as they say."

"Eugene hit you awfully hard."

Rocky seemed to have sobered up some. "You know that was a grave I found, don't you?"

McCall said nothing.

"I know I said I thought it was old, but it wasn't. And it wasn't no Indian grave like Eugene was saying, and I think you know that, too."

She patted his shoulder. "Get some rest." As she turned toward her pickup, all she wanted was to go home and put this day behind her.

But as she drove the few miles out of town and turned down the river road to her small old cabin beside the Milk River, she saw the pickup parked in her yard.

She slowed as she recognized the logo on the side of the truck. Montana Fish, Wildlife and Parks. She felt her heart drop as she pulled alongside and Game Warden Luke Crawford climbed out.

LUKE HATED THE WAY HE FELT as he watched McCall walk toward him. He was again that awkward, tongue-tied, infatuated seventeen-year-old—just as he'd been the first time he'd ever kissed McCall Winchester.

A lot of things had changed in the years since, but not that.

"Luke?" She stopped in front of her pickup. One hand rested on her hip just above the grip of her weapon. She was still in uniform except for her hat. Some of her long dark hair had come loose from the clip at the nape of her neck and now fell over one shoulder.

He tipped his hat. "Sorry to bother you."

She frowned, clearly waiting for him to tell her what the hell he was doing here. She had to have heard he was back in town.

"I got another call tonight about some poaching down in the river bottom," he said.

"On my property?"

He pointed down into the thicket of tangled willows and cottonwoods. "On the place down the river, but I believe they used the river road to get in and out so they had to have gone right past your place. I was wondering if you heard anything last night? Would have probably been between two and four this morning."

"I pulled the late shift last night so I wasn't around. Sorry."

He nodded and asked who else knew her schedule.

"You saying the poachers knew I would be gone last night?"

"It crossed my mind. Your place is the closest."

She leaned against the front of her pickup, clearly not intending to ask him inside. The Little Rockies in the distance were etched a deep purple against the twilight. He noticed in the waning light that she looked exhausted.

"Rough day?" he asked, feeling the cool air come up out of the river bottom.

"You could say that." She was studying him, waiting as if she expected him to tell her the real reason he was here.

But he'd said everything years ago and she hadn't believed him then. No reason she'd believe him now.

He closed his notebook. "I'd appreciate it if you kept an eye out and gave me a call if you see or hear anything."

She pushed herself off the front of her pickup. "You bet."

"The poachers are driving a pickup, probably a half ton or three-quarter-ton four-wheel drive."

"Like half the residents in this county," she said.

"Narrows it right down for me." He smiled, hat in his hand, thinking that even as exhausted as McCall was she'd never looked more beautiful. He told himself to just get in his truck and get out of there before he said something he'd regret.

She smiled, a tired almost sad smile. "Well, I hope you catch 'em."

"Me, too." He put on his hat, tipped it, and turned toward his pickup. As he slid behind the wheel, he saw that she'd gone inside her cabin. The lights glowed golden through the windows. He sat for a moment, wishing—

Mentally he gave himself a swift kick and started the truck, annoyed for going down that old trail of thought. From the beginning he and McCall hadn't stood a chance, not with the bad blood between their families. He'd been a fool to think that they did.

But for a while, she'd made him believe they were destined to be together, star-crossed lovers who'd found a way. They'd been young and foolish. At least he had, he thought as he left.

He didn't dare glance back, knowing he was wasting his time if he thought she cared a plugged nickel for him.

If he had looked back, though, he would have seen her standing in the deepening shadows of her deck, hugging herself against the cool of the night, watching him drive away.

Chapter Four

The next morning, McCall woke blurry-eyed to the sound of a vehicle driving up in her yard. She pulled on her robe and padded out to the living room as she heard someone coming across the deck, making a beeline for her front door.

It was too early for company. Had something happened?

She thought of Luke. Not him again, she hoped. Seeing him waiting for her last night had been the last straw after the day she'd had. She'd had a devil of a time getting to sleep last night and it was all Luke Crawford's fault. What the hell was he doing back in Whitehorse, anyway?

Usually, she found peace in her cabin on the river. The place was small, but the view from her deck made up for it. She loved to sit and listen to the rustle of the cottonwood trees, watch the deer meander through the tall grass along the river's edge and breathe in the sweet scents of the seasons.

Last night, though, after she'd watched Luke drive away, not even a beer and a hot bath had soothed what ailed her.

Now she realized she hadn't locked the door last night. The knob turned, and out of the corner of her eye, she saw her father's hunting license on the kitchen counter where she'd left it last night.

She quickly snatched up the license and, lifting the lid on an empty canister on the counter, dropped it inside.

She'd barely dropped the lid, when the door was flung open.

"What in the world?" she bellowed as her mother came busting in.

Her mother stopped in midstride, a cigarette dangling from one corner of her mouth. "Did I forget to knock?"

"Do you know what time it is?" McCall demanded. "What are you doing here?"

"I had to see you before I went to work," her mother snapped back. "You might remember I work early."

Before McCall could wonder what was so important that it had her mother here at the crack of dawn, Ruby enlightened her.

"I can't believe you went out to the Winchesters'. What were you thinking?" her mother demanded. "Now that old woman is threatening to have you arrested? It's all over town."

McCall leaned against the kitchen counter. "Why is it that anything I do is always all over town within minutes?"

Ruby waved a hand through the air as if it was too obvious. "You're a *Winchester*."

McCall sighed. "Only by name." A name she'd often regretted.

"You're *Trace* Winchester's *daughter*."

As if that were something to celebrate, McCall thought, but was smart enough not to voice that sentiment to her mother, especially in the mood Ruby was in. No matter what Trace had done to her, Ruby would defend him to her death.

"As *Trace* Winchester's daughter, I should have the right to visit my grandmother," McCall said instead and motioned at her mother's cigarette. She didn't permit smoking in her cabin. Not after inhaling her mother's secondhand smoke for years.

"Don't you want to know how I found out?" Ruby asked, looking around for an ashtray.

"Not particularly."

"That bitch Enid. She must have called everyone in town this morning, announcing that her boss was going to have you arrested."

"I wasn't arrested." But she could be soon for interfering in a murder investigation. She tried not to think about that right now, though.

Ruby, not seeing an ashtray, opened the cabin door and started to flick the cigarette out, then apparently thought better of it.

"That old harpy," she said, stepping outside and leaving the door open as she ground the cigarette into the dirt. "I thought she'd be dead by now. She's got to be a hundred. Mean to the core."

McCall poured yesterday's coffee into two mugs, put them in the microwave and handed her mother a cup as she came back in. Taking the other cup, McCall curled up on one end of the couch.

The coffee tasted terrible, but it was hot and she needed the caffeine. Her mother sat down at the opposite end of the couch. She seemed to have calmed down a little.

"I just don't understand why you would go out there after all these years?"

"Maybe I finally wanted to see my grandmother."

Ruby eyed her. "Just like that?"

"Just like that."

"And?"

"And I saw her. End of story."

"Did she even know who you were? Of course she did. One look at you and she'd see the Winchester in you."

"You never told me I looked so much like her." She hadn't meant it to sound so accusatory.

Ruby shrugged and took a sip of her coffee. Her mother was so used to drinking bad coffee she didn't even grimace. "So what did she say to you?"

"It was a short conversation before she showed me the door."

Ruby toyed with the handle on her coffee mug. "Are you going to see her again?"

Was she worried McCall would be accepted by the Winchesters when Ruby hadn't been? The idea would have been laughable if it hadn't hurt so much.

"She called the sheriff on me. Does that answer your question?"

Ruby was ablaze, cursing Pepper Winchester clear to Hades and back, not that it was anything new.

"I'm sorry, baby," her mother said. She finished her coffee and got up to rinse the mug in the kitchen sink. "But don't feel too bad. It isn't like she was close to any of her kids or her other grandkids. She's just an evil old crone who deserves to live like a hermit."

McCall didn't tell her mother that she felt a little sorry for Pepper Winchester—anyone who'd seen the hope in her eyes at the mention of Trace's name would have been.

Ruby checked her watch. "I'm going to be late for work." She looked at her daughter as if she held McCall responsible. "Promise me you won't go back out there."

McCall was saved by the ringing of her cell phone. She found it where she'd dropped it last night and checked caller ID. "It's my boss."

"Then you'd better take it," Ruby said. "Stop by the café later."

"If I can," McCall said and waited until her mother disappeared out the door before she took the call, fearing that her morning was about to get worse.

"You're up early," Buzz Crawford said from the deck of his lake house as Luke joined him.

"Haven't you heard? Poachers never sleep."

Buzz chuckled. "You're right about that. Catch any lately?"

He'd spent the night down in the river bottom patrolling. He wouldn't have been able to sleep anyway after his visit to McCall. This morning he'd caught a few hours' sleep before coming by his uncle's.

"A few," he said, distracted at the thought of McCall.

Buzz shook his head. "You're too easy on the bastards. These guys around here aren't afraid of you. When I was warden, they knew if they broke the law I'd be on them like stink on a dog."

Luke had heard it all before, way too many times.

"So how's the fishing been?" he asked to change the subject. It was one of those rare April days when the temperature was already in the fifties and expected to get up as high as seventy before the day was over. The sky overhead was a brilliant blue, cloudless and bright with the morning sun.

Buzz, who was sitting in one of the lawn chairs over-looking Nelson Reservoir, said something under his breath Luke didn't catch and was thankful for it.

"Help yourself to some coffee, if you want," Buzz said, handing Luke his cup to refill.

"Thanks." Luke stepped into the kitchen and poured himself a mug, refilling his uncle's before returning to the deck.

A flock of geese honked somewhere in the distance and he could see the dark V of a half-dozen pelicans circling over the water. The ice had only melted off last week leaving the water a deep green.

"Walleye chop," Buzz said as Luke handed him his coffee, indicating the water's surface now being kicked up by the wind. "The fish'll be bitin'. Since you're not going to catch any criminals anyway, you might as well come fishing with me."

Luke ignored the dig. "Can't." But spending the day fishing did have its appeal. "I have to work on the house or it will never get finished." He had a couple of days off, and he planned to get as much done as possible.

"I've never understood why you bought that place back," Buzz said, shaking his head. "It was nothing but work for your father. I'd think you'd want to start fresh. No ghosts."

Is that how Buzz saw the past? Full of ghosts? It surprised Luke. The old homestead was his mother's family's place. He'd lived there his first seven years with his parents before their deaths and cherished those memories.

"You hear about those bones found south of town?" his uncle asked, then swore when Luke said he hadn't. "You never know what's going on," Buzz complained. "Anyway, it seems Rocky Harrison found some bones and was going on about them at the bar and somehow Eugene got arrested."

No mystery there, Luke thought. Eugene getting arrested had long ceased to be news.

"Rocky swore the bones were human. Probably just some dead animal. I thought for sure you might have heard somethin'."

Luke watched a fishing boat against the opposite shore, the putter of the motor lulling him as he wondered idly why his uncle would be so interested in some old bones.

PEPPER STOPPED IN FRONT of Trace's bedroom door, the key clutched in her hand. She'd had Enid lock the room, wanting it left just as it was the day her youngest son left it.

Had she really thought he'd return to the ranch? He'd been a day short of twenty the last time she saw him. He'd promised to come to the birthday party she was throwing for him. All of the family would be there and had been warned to be on their best behavior. She had planned the huge party and, even though the two of them had fought, Pepper had been so sure he wouldn't miss his party for anything.

"You old fool," she muttered as she slipped the key into the lock. She'd had her first child at seventeen. Trace had come along unexpectedly after her doctor said she couldn't have any more children. She had thought of Trace as her miracle child.

She realized she hadn't thought about her other children and grandchildren in years. They'd resented Trace and her relationship with him. Their jealousy had turned her stomach and finally turned her against them.

With a grimace, she realized she could be a great-grandmother by now.

The door to Trace's room opened. Air wafted out, smelling stale and musty and she could see dust thick as paint everywhere as she stepped in.

The bed was covered in an old quilt, the colors faded, the stitching broken in dozens of places. She started to touch the once-vibrant colored squares but pulled her hand back.

Her eyes lit on the stack of outdoor and hunting magazines piled up beside the bed. Trace had lived and breathed hunting. He'd been like his father that way.

Her husband, Call, came to mind. She chased that memory away like a pesky fly, wishing she could kill it.

The door to the closet was open, and she could see most of Trace's clothes still hanging inside it, also covered with dust just like his guitar in the corner, like his high school sports trophies lined up on the shelves and his wild animal posters on the walls.

Pepper stood in the middle of the room feeling weak and angry at herself for that weakness. No wonder she had avoided this room, like so many others, all these years.

But as she stood there, she realized there was nothing of Trace left here. There was no reason to lock the room anymore or to keep what her son had left behind.

Trace Winchester was gone and he wasn't coming back.

That realization struck her to her core since she'd held on to the opposite belief for the past twenty-seven years.

Tears blurred her eyes as she looked around the room realizing what had changed. She'd become convinced her son was never coming home the moment she'd laid eyes on his deputy daughter.

MCCALL MENTALLY KICKED herself for the position she'd put herself in as she pulled into the sheriff's department parking lot. If she'd told the sheriff up front about what she'd found and her suspicions—

When he'd called this morning, he hadn't said why he wanted to see her, just that he did, even though it was her day off. He had only said it was important.

The best thing she could do was confess all.

Except as she got out of her pickup, she knew she couldn't do that. Not yet. Once she told Grant about the hunting license, the news would be all over town.

Right now she had a slim advantage to find the killer because he didn't know she was after him yet.

Even if the killer—who she was assuming still lived in Whitehorse since few people left—had heard about the discovery of the bones, he would still think he was safe. He'd taken everything that identified the body—even her father's boots, his wallet, his pickup and rifle—all things that could have identified the body.

The killer just hadn't known about the hunting license in one of Trace's pockets, apparently.

As McCall started toward her boss's office, she hesitated. She was jeopardizing more than her job by investigating this on her own. Once she started asking questions around town, the killer would know she was on to him and she would be putting her life in danger.

But if there was even a chance that Trace Winchester wouldn't have run out on them, that he'd have stayed and made them a family, then she owed it to all of them to find out who had taken that away.

"Thanks for coming in," Sheriff Grant Sheridan said as she tapped on his open door. He motioned to a chair in front of his desk. "Please close the door."

She stepped in, shutting the door behind her. Grant leaned back in his chair. He was a stocky, reasonably attractive man, with dark hair graying at the temples, intense blue eyes and a permanent grave expression.

A contemporary of her mother's, McCall had heard that the two had once dated back in high school, but then who hadn't her mother dated?

"How are you this morning?" Grant asked as McCall sat.

"Fine." She hoped this wasn't about her visit yesterday to the Winchester Ranch but maybe that was better than the alternative.

"I talked to the crime lab this morning," he said, not sounding happy about it.

She felt her heart drop. The DNA couldn't have come back already. But Grant could have heard about the unauthorized test.

"I've asked them to put a rush on those remains you sent them," Grant said.

"A rush?" she echoed. She'd thought she'd have time. Now, her undercover sleuthing aside, once the sheriff found out about the DNA test and the hunting license she'd be lucky to still have a job. Worse, she could end up in jail.

"After what happened at the bar last night, I had to speed up the process," Grant was saying. "Apparently Rocky, with the help of Eugene Crawford, got a bunch from out on the reservation all worked up. They're convinced one of their ancestor's grave has been disturbed."

"It wasn't an Indian grave."

"You're sure?"

"Positive." She wished Rocky had kept his fool mouth shut, but it was too late for that. "Along with the bones, I found shirt snaps, metal buttons off a pair of jeans and what was left of a leather belt."

"So it was a grave," Grant said, sounding surprised. "I thought it was just bones."

He hadn't asked her and he hadn't been around when she'd mailed everything off to the crime lab. At least that was her excuse for keeping more than the hunting license from him.

His being distracted for weeks now had made it too easy. Now everything hinged on that DNA report from the crime lab.

"When you said the bones were human, I just assumed they'd been there for a while," Grant said now. "How old are we talking?"

"Hard to say." Remains deteriorated at different rates depending on the time of year, the weather, the soil and how deep the body was buried.

"More than fifty years?"

"Less, I'd say."

He was silent for a long moment. "Where exactly were these bones found again?"

She told him.

He grew even quieter before he said, "Thanks for taking care of Rocky last night. We're still holding Eugene Crawford. I understand he got into it with you. Are you all right?"

"He didn't hurt me."

"But he apparently grabbed you and shoved you?"

"He was drunk and looking for a fight," she said. "I didn't see any reason to make more of it than it was."

Grant studied her for a moment before nodding. "Well, good job at keeping a lid on things. It could have been much worse if you hadn't acted as quickly as you did. It wouldn't be the first time Eugene Crawford tore up a bar." He glanced at his watch, sighed and stood, signaling that they were finished.

McCall tried to hide her relief.

"We should have the results from the lab on those bones in a week," Grant was saying. "In the meantime, I think it would be best if we said as little as possible about the discovery, don't you agree?"

She did indeed. She couldn't help but wonder how he'd feel when he found out just whose bones they really were. If he thought there was trouble now, wait until he had to deal with Pepper Winchester.

One week. When the report came back with the DNA test, all hell would break loose. She'd give up the hunting license and let the chips fall where they may. But in the meantime, she planned to make the most of it.

LUKE GLANCED OVER AT HIS UNCLE, worried. Buzz didn't seem to be taking to retirement well after thirty-five years as a Montana game warden. While he swore that he was content fishing most every day, Luke suspected he missed catching bad guys.

Buzz, who'd made a name for himself as one of the most hard-nosed game wardens in the west, had been written up in a couple of major metropolitan newspapers and magazines, helping make him a legend in these parts.

"Did Eugene get out of jail?" Luke asked into the silence that had stretched between them.

"I'm going in this afternoon to bail him out. It was the soonest they'd release him." Buzz swore under his breath. "You know who arrested him, don't you?" Luke felt his stomach clench. "McCall Winchester. The Winchesters have always had it in for our family."

And vice versa, Luke thought, but was smart enough not to say it.

"Eugene said he hit you up for that money he owes for gambling debts," his uncle said after a moment.

Was that accusation he heard in Buzz's voice? "He needs fifty thousand dollars. I can't raise that kind of money."

"He asked you for that much? When he came to me it was only thirty." Buzz swore. "He tell you anything about these guys he owes the money to?"

"No." But Luke could imagine.

"He seems to think they won't find him here. Or maybe he thinks we'll protect him." Buzz had always protected his son, to Eugene's detriment. Luke saw there was both regret and determination in his uncle's expression. "I don't have the money to give him either."

Luke wasn't sure where this conversation was headed. "He has to stop gambling, get a job—"

"Don't you think I know that?" Buzz snapped. "But fifty thousand? It would take him years to make that much at a job in Whitehorse. Meanwhile, these guys aren't going to wait on their money."

Luke shook his head, hating the desperation he heard in his uncle's voice. Eugene would be even more desperate and probably do something crazy, knowing his cousin.

"I need to get going," Luke said finishing his coffee and rising to take the mug back into the kitchen.

As he came back out, he heard the sound of a vehicle engine. Shielding his eyes from the sun, he saw a white pickup pull in, a sheriff's department emblem on the side and a set of lights on top.

Luke heard his uncle swear as Deputy Sheriff McCall Winchester climbed out.

Chapter Five

McCall had hoped to catch Buzz Crawford alone. The last person she wanted to see was Luke. But unfortunately as she pulled up to the lake house, his pickup was parked outside.

No way to make a graceful escape even if she could let the coward in her win out.

As she neared the house, she saw the two Crawford men on the deck, Luke standing as if about to leave and Buzz sprawled in a lawn chair as if he didn't have a care in the world.

She stopped at the bottom of the stairs to the deck, shading her eyes to take in the two. It hadn't escaped her notice last night that Luke had changed. He'd filled out, looking stronger, definitely confident and as always, handsome in an understated, very male way.

She could see that Luke didn't like the idea of leaving her alone with his uncle given the family history. Of course he would be protective of the uncle who'd raised him and by now he would also know about his cousin's arrest last night and who Buzz would blame.

McCall smiled to herself at the indecision she saw

in Luke's expression. But was he afraid to leave her alone with Buzz because of his fear of what his uncle might do? Or her?

"I'd like to speak to Buzz alone," McCall said flashing her badge. She heard Buzz curse loud enough for her to hear.

"You coming out to arrest me as well as my son?" Buzz snapped.

Luke started down the steps to the shore. As he stepped past McCall, he said under his breath, "You sure this is a good idea?"

"I can handle Buzz." The nearness of Luke Crawford was a whole other story, she thought as he brushed on past her.

"And I can handle the deputy," Buzz said from his lawn chair.

McCall listened to the crunch of Luke's boot heels on the rocky shore before ascending the stairs to the deck.

Buzz was a big beefy man with ham-sized fists and a predilection for violence—much like his son Eugene. As the former county game warden, he'd made more than his share of enemies since he had a reputation for being a heartless bastard who would have arrested his own mother.

McCall had heard stories about him roughing up poachers, claiming they'd resisted arrest when they swore they hadn't.

"What do you want?" Buzz demanded scowling at her now as he got up and went through the open door into his house.

She stepped cautiously to the doorway and peered into the dim darkness.

The place wasn't much larger than her cabin on the river and even more sparsely furnished. The only thing on the walls other than deer and antelope mounts were framed yellowed articles from newspapers and magazines featuring Buzz when he was a game warden.

He saw her looking at the write-ups about him and chuckled. "That's what a real officer of the law looks like," he boasted as he poured himself a mug of coffee but he didn't offer her one.

She saw that he'd changed since he'd left his game warden job. He wasn't in shape anymore and he'd aged. She thought retirement wasn't working out so well for him.

"So what brings a Winchester out to see me?" Buzz asked, glaring at her.

She smiled, wondering at this hatred between the Crawfords and Winchesters. It made no sense. Especially when aimed at her since no one in town considered her a Winchester—including the Winchester family.

"I'm here about Trace Winchester's disappearance," she said into the cold malevolent silence.

Buzz had started to take a drink of the hot coffee, but jerked back at her words, spilling some on the floor and burning his mouth. He swore and put down the cup.

"Your name keeps coming up in my investigation," she said. "I was wondering why that was."

"No mystery there," Buzz spat. "Your old man kept breaking the law and I kept catching him."

"How many times was that?"

He shrugged. "I lost track."

"Really? You were the only game warden for this entire county back then. You alone had an area the size of Massachusetts to cover, from Canada to the Missouri

River Breaks. It would have been impossible to catch Trace Winchester every time he broke the law unless you made it a personal vendetta."

"Maybe he was just stupid and got caught a lot."

"Maybe. I guess it would depend on how many times you arrested him and for what."

She'd checked the arrests before she'd driven out. They were public record. "Let's see," she said taking the list from her pocket. "Littering, trespassing, improper boat safety equipment…" She looked up. "You wrote him far more tickets than you wrote anyone else in the county."

Buzz looked uneasy.

"It makes me wonder just what your relationship was with my father."

"Relationship? I couldn't stand the little—" He caught himself. "Trace Winchester was a spoiled kid who thought he was above the law. I was a law enforcement officer. You should be able to understand that."

She nodded as she stuffed the list back into her pocket and took out her notebook and pen. "When was the last time you saw Trace?"

Buzz picked up his mug again and took a sip of coffee, letting her wait. "Hell if I know. Whatever date I ticketed his worthless ass."

"You never saw him again? Like say the next morning?" she asked, her gaze riveted to his.

He stared right back. "That's right."

"You're sure about that? You didn't by any chance wait for him on a ridge south of town?" Was it her imagination or did she see fear contract his eyes?

"You deaf? I already told you. Quit wasting my time."

"What exactly is your problem with the Winchester family?"

He blinked in surprise. "Why don't you ask your mother. Or your grandmother. Oh, that's right, Pepper disowned you."

"Actually, I don't think she went to the trouble."

He sneered at that. "Your grandfather cheated my brother out of some land. Call Winchester was a crook and a liar."

"Call's been dead for more than forty years. What did that have to do with my mother? Or my father other than he was a Winchester and spoiled?"

"I didn't say it had anything to do with your father." His smile was as sharp as the filet knife lying on the counter next to him. "If you want to know what it has to do with your mother, well, I suggest you ask her."

McCall studied Buzz for a moment, hoping he wasn't another of her mother's old boyfriends. "What happened to my father's rifle?"

Buzz jerked back as if she'd taken a swing at him. "How the hell should I know? I would imagine he took if with him when he left town."

"How is that possible? You arrested him the day before for—" she made a show pulling out her list and checking it again "—poaching an antelope before opening season. If the rifle had been used in the commission of a crime, the weapon would have been considered evidence and confiscated under the law. So you must have taken it, right?"

Buzz looked worried. "No. Maybe Trace hid it. Or

maybe I just forgot. I can't remember. But if I had taken it, the rifle would still be locked up in evidence."

"I checked. It's not. Anyway, my mother swears that Trace had the rifle the next morning when he left the house to go hunting. A model 99 Savage rifle with his father's initials carved in the stock."

"You'd take the word of your mother?"

She studied him, feeling an icy chill at the malice she saw in his eyes.

Her mother had said Trace might have had something on Buzz he used as leverage to keep his rifle, but why the obvious hated for her mother?

"Was my father blackmailing you?"

Buzz went to slam his mug down on the counter but missed. The mug hit the floor, shattering. Coffee shot out in an arc across the tile, making a dark stain at his feet.

She saw he was shaking all over, even his voice. "Get out of my house. I'm done talking to you without my lawyer."

McCall closed her notebook, put it and her pen away before she stepped back into the sunlight on the deck. Even the early morning sun felt good after the cold inside.

"One more thing," she said sticking her head back into the house.

He seemed shocked she was still on his property and had the audacity to ask him another question.

"Did I mention Rocky Harrison found a human grave south of town on a high ridge from a spot where you can see the Winchester Ranch in the distance?"

Buzz didn't move, didn't speak, didn't even seem to breathe. It wasn't the reaction she'd hoped for but it was a reaction.

"What the hell does that have to do with me?" he finally demanded.

She shrugged. "When I know that, I'll be back. Keep your lawyer's number handy."

LUKE COULDN'T HELP BEING distracted as he filed his report on the poaching incidents. Seeing McCall Winchester again had thrown him, especially since her visit to his uncle this morning had looked official and that worried him.

As he was hanging up from making his report, he got a call from a friend in the Helena Fish and Game office.

"Something going on up there with your uncle Buzz?" his friend George asked. "A deputy by the name of McCall Winchester has been looking into some of Buzz's old cases. You know anything about this?"

Luke swore under his breath. "No, what cases are we talking about?"

"Mostly those involving a Trace Winchester. Any relation to the deputy?"

"Trace Winchester was her father. He disappeared before she was born almost thirty years ago."

"Probably not strange then that she's looking into those cases," George said. "She's probably just curious. But there were quite a few tickets issued. Her father must have been a real troublemaker."

Luke wondered about that. He'd heard rumors about Trace Winchester but had figured the man's exploits had been greatly exaggerated.

"Apparently," Luke agreed, his worry increasing. He'd thought Buzz was acting strangely this morning because of Eugene's arrest and the gambling trouble. Now he wasn't so sure.

"I thought I'd let you know, anyway."

"I appreciate that." He hung up, wondering what McCall had wanted with his uncle. Why, after all these years, would she be looking into some old fish and game violations against her father?

More to the point, was she just fishing? Or had she caught something that could mean trouble for Buzz?

MCCALL COULDN'T SHAKE OFF the feeling as she left that Buzz was lying about something. She'd definitely rattled him.

While she was trying hard not to let her dislike of Buzz Crawford overly influence her one-woman unauthorized investigation, it was odd that he hadn't confiscated her father's hunting rifle. Odder still were some of his reactions.

The missing rifle seemed the key, she thought as she saw Red Harper's pickup parked in front of the Cowboy Bar.

Red Harper, according to what she'd heard, had been her father's former hunting buddy and best friend.

Red was one of those people born into a family with money *and* a good name. His father owned several farm implement dealerships across the state and had left Red a large thriving ranch north of town.

As McCall parked, she could see Red having an early lunch at the counter. If anyone would know what had been going on with her father the day he died, it should be his best friend.

The smell of stale beer and floor cleaner hit her as

McCall entered the dim bar. It was early enough that only a few of the regulars were occupying the stools along the bar.

"Red," she said by way of greeting as she neared his stool.

He gave her a nod, already wary. She assumed it was the uniform. According to stories she'd heard, Red had been a lot like her father in his younger days, both from money, both unable to keep trouble from finding them.

The difference was that Red had grown up.

Trace Winchester never got the chance.

"Buy you a beer?" she asked but didn't give him time to answer as she motioned to the bartender to bring them two of whatever he was having.

"Mind if we move over to a table?" she asked. "I'd like to talk with you."

He pushed away his plate, his burger finished, and got to his feet, although he didn't look anxious to talk to her. "What's this about?"

She took a table away from the regulars at the bar and sat down. Red reluctantly joined her.

"If this is about your mother and me—"

"My mother?" McCall couldn't help the surprise in her voice. Red Harper was one of the only men her mother's age who hadn't dated her after Trace had allegedly left town.

McCall had always wondered why.

"Your mother didn't tell you I asked her out?"

She shook her head. That too was strange. McCall had lived her mother's ups and downs with men and was always the first to hear when a new man came into Ruby's life—or left it.

"Sorry, but no. Ruby can take care of herself." If only that were true. McCall had seen her mother go through so many relationships that were obviously doomed from the beginning that she didn't try to warn her off certain men anymore.

McCall, though, couldn't help but wonder why Red had decided to ask her mother out now.

Their beers arrived. When the bartender left again, McCall picked up the frosty glass and took a sip of the icy cold beer.

Red seemed to relax a little. "So what's this about?"

"I just wanted to ask you about my dad. You probably knew him better than anyone."

He nodded and picked up his drink. "There was no one like Trace."

"Is it true he was as wild as people say?"

Red smiled, flushing a little. He was a handsome man with a full head of reddish-blond hair still free of gray, blue eyes and a great smile. McCall had always liked him.

"There's some truth to the stories." Red chuckled ruefully. "He was a good guy, though. He just liked to do what he wanted. He and I were a lot alike that way."

She took another drink of her beer and waited for Red to continue.

"He liked to fish and hunt and drink and chase women." Red seemed to realize what he'd said and quickly added, "Well, until your mother."

McCall had caught his slip-up. Why hadn't she thought that there might have been another woman in her father's life?

Ruby had been pregnant with McCall, wildly hormonal,

according to her, and jealous as hell, if her other relationships were any indication.

Her mother's life was straight out of a country-and-western song. If there had been another woman in Trace Winchester's life, McCall shuddered to think how far her mother might have gone to make sure no woman took her man.

Red finished his beer in a hurry, realizing he'd messed up. "I'm sorry, but I have an appointment and really need to get going."

"Why *haven't* you asked my mother out before now?"

He looked startled by the question.

"Trace has been gone for twenty-seven years," she said.

Red smiled ruefully. "Gone, but not forgotten." He shook his head. "Couldn't compete, not with her expecting him to come back at any moment."

McCall realized that Red had been competing with a ghost, even if he hadn't known Trace was dead.

"You'd be good for Ruby," she said.

He smiled at that. "Another strike against me. But thanks for saying so."

As McCall came out of the bar, blinking at the bright sunlight, she found Luke Crawford leaning against his pickup, obviously waiting for her.

"McCall," he said with a tip of his hat.

She realized at once that he'd gotten wind of her digging into Trace's old arrests for poaching and other hunting violations.

Not that she wasn't surprised to see him.

Was it always going to be like this? Her heart taking off just at the sight of him? Looking for him every time she came into town, afraid he would just appear as he had now and catch her off guard?

He'd been gone for the past ten years—since they'd both graduated from high school. The ten years apart hadn't changed how she felt. All the hurt, humiliation and heartbreak were still there at just the sight of him.

"Been waitin' long?" she asked.

"Kind of early to be drinking," Luke joked.

She knew she must smell like the bar, a combination of old cigarette smoke and stale beer. Even with Montana bars going nonsmoking it would take years for the odor to go away inside some establishments.

"You haven't been waiting out here because you're worried about my drinking habits," she said, realizing someone in the state Fish and Game Department had to have tipped him off.

"This is awkward," he said. "I heard that you're looking into a few old poaching cases involving your father."

She bristled. While all law enforcement in this part of Montana helped each other when there was trouble, this was none of his business. "Do you have a problem with that?"

"If you're targeting my uncle for some reason it is."

Well, it was finally out in the open.

"Why? Do you think he has something to hide?"

Luke shook his head as if disgusted. She saw his jaw muscle tighten and realized he was trying to control his temper.

"Look," he said finally, "the trouble with our families was a long time ago—"

"My father disappeared twenty-seven years ago—the day after your uncle ticketed him."

Luke blinked. "You're blaming Buzz for your father skipping town? Buzz was just doing his job."

"Was he? I think Buzz Crawford's reputation speaks for itself."

"What the hell is that supposed to mean?"

She sighed. "Come on, Luke. You wouldn't have been out here waiting for me if you weren't worried that your uncle is guilty of something. You know Buzz. That's why you're concerned. That's why my checking on some of his old arrests has you waiting outside a bar for me."

"Buzz took his job seriously. There is nothing wrong with that."

She met his gaze. His eyes were a warm deep brown, his thick hair dark, much like her own. Like her, he had some Native American ancestry in his blood.

McCall remembered one time when a substitute grade school teacher had broken up a fight between Luke and another boy.

"All right, you little Apache, knock it off," the teacher had said, grabbing Luke by the scruff of his neck.

"I'm Chippewa," he'd said indignantly as she returned him to his seat.

McCall had remembered the pride in his voice and felt guilty because she had never taken pride in her own ancestry. But how could she with a father like Trace Winchester, the man everyone believed had deserted his pregnant wife and unborn child? Not to mention her grandmother, who denied McCall's very existence.

"Look, I've always hated the hostility between our families," Luke said now. "I don't want to see it stirred up all over again."

She would have liked to have told him that this had

nothing to do with whatever problems there'd been between the two of them—or their families, but she wasn't sure of that.

"I know my uncle can be difficult, but he took me in and raised me when my parents died. I owe him. If he's in some kind of trouble…"

"It's sheriff's department business." The second time she'd lied today, but certainly not likely to be a record the way things were going. She started to step past him.

He grabbed her arm. His fingers on her flesh were like a branding iron. She flinched and he immediately let go.

"Sorry," he said, holding up his hand as if in surrender.

She said nothing, still stunned that Luke's touch could have that effect on her after all these years.

He took a step back, looking as shaken as she felt. Was it possible she wasn't the only one who'd felt it?

PEPPER WINCHESTER HADN'T been able to rest since McCall's visit. She hated the way she felt, her fear making her weak. She hated feeling weak, and worse, no longer in control.

"You should drink this," Enid said, appearing with a tray. On it was a glass of juice. "It will make you feel better."

Pepper knew there would be something in the juice that would make all this go away for a while. She and Enid had never talked about the drugs the housekeeper had been slipping her over the past twenty-seven years.

At first Pepper had been grateful, wanting to escape from her thoughts, her memories, the things she'd said and done, especially in regard to her son Trace.

She took the glass from the tray and turned back to

the window where she'd been standing when Enid had sneaked up on her.

She'd never questioned why Enid drugged her. No doubt to make less work for herself and her husband, Alfred. Whatever Enid put into her juice had always knocked her out for at least twenty-four hours, sometimes more.

It would have been so easy to down the juice and let herself surrender to that peaceful nothingness state.

"I'll drink it after I have a little something to eat," Pepper said. "Perhaps a sandwich. Have we any turkey?"

"I've got some ham." Enid didn't sound happy about having to go back to the kitchen to make a sandwich and bring it all the way back up. "You should have eaten the breakfast I made you."

That was another problem with the drugs Enid gave her. They had allowed the power to shift from boss to employee over the years. Enid acted as if this were her house.

Turning to face her housekeeper, Pepper considered the elderly woman standing before her. Her first instinct was to fire her and her worthless husband. But she couldn't bear the thought of having to hire strangers and she couldn't go without help.

"Why don't I come down to the kitchen for the sandwich," Pepper said. "It will save you the extra trip."

Enid studied her for a moment, looking a little uneasy. "Whatever you want. I'm just here to make sure you're taken care of."

Yes, Pepper thought, wondering at how Enid had taken care of her and what she and her husband might have planned in the future. She realized she might not be safe. Especially if Enid thought for a moment that

Pepper might ever reconcile with her children and grandchildren.

While there was no chance of that, McCall's visit might have the housekeeper and husband worried. Pepper saw now that she would have to be very careful from now on.

Later she would pretend to drink the juice but surreptitiously pour it down the drain. While her hired help thought she was asleep perhaps she would do some sneaking around of her own.

Chapter Six

Determined to put Luke Crawford out of her mind, McCall concentrated on what Red had hinted at—that her father had a girlfriend. If anyone would have known, it was the woman her mother had worked with twenty-seven years ago.

Patty Mason had been slinging hash as long as Ruby Bates Winchester. The two had worked together from the time they were teenagers until about the time McCall was born.

Patty had gone to work at the Hi-Line Café and it was there that McCall found her after the lunch crowd had cleared out. Patty was the opposite of Ruby. While Ruby was skin and bone, Patty was round and plump with bulbous cheeks.

She smiled as McCall came in and took a seat at one of the empty booths. "Just coffee, please, and if you have a minute, join me."

Patty glanced around the empty café and laughed before pouring two cups and bringing them to the table. She squeezed into the booth, kicked off her shoes, put her feet up on the seat and leaned back against the wall.

"This is the first second I've had to put my aching dogs up all day," Patty said, wiggling her toes. "So how you doin', girl? How's your mama? I never see her anymore. Hell, probably cuz we both work all the time."

"Ruby's good." As good as Ruby ever got, McCall thought.

"She seeing anyone?" Patty was on her third marriage, this time to an elderly rancher. They had a place to the north of town on the road to Canada.

"Red Harper." This came as no surprise, McCall saw, since Patty would have already heard through the Whitehorse grapevine. McCall was the only one out of the loop apparently.

"You know I always thought she and Red would end up together," Patty said with a chuckle. "Sure has taken him long enough though, huh."

McCall's thought exactly. "I was hoping you could help me with something," she said, getting right to the point. "Were you working with Ruby the morning Trace disappeared?"

Patty slid her feet from the booth seat and sat up, blinking. "My goodness, girl, that was so long ago."

"Ruby said she was working the early shift."

"That's right. You know I *do* remember. It was a crazy day. We got in a busload of Canadians down here for a whist tournament." She frowned. "Wow, how many years ago was that now?"

"Twenty-seven."

"My memory is better than I thought." Patty grinned. "I remember because your mama came in late. I really had my hands full. I knew she was sick, being pregnant with you and all, but I was so mad at her."

"Did she say why she was late?" McCall asked.

"She was all rattled, you know how she gets. It was plain as her face that she and Trace had had another fight. I wondered if she'd been to bed at all the night before, everything considered, you know?"

McCall didn't know. "Such as?"

"Well…" Patty looked uncomfortable. "The way she looked. She'd been crying and that old pickup she drove… It was covered in mud. I asked her where the devil she'd been since your mama wasn't one for driving much, especially on these roads around here when they're wet."

McCall thought of the road into the ridge south of town. "And what did she say?"

"Said Trace borrowed her truck." Patty mugged a face. "I knew that wasn't true. He never drove anything but that pretty new black Chevy his mama bought him as a bribe to leave Ruby. He took a perverse satisfaction into getting that truck dirty and staying with Ruby just to show his mama he couldn't be bought."

McCall had wondered where Trace had gotten the pickup. Now she knew. Her dear grandmother.

"So where do you think Ruby had been in her pickup?"

Patty shook her head. "You could ask her."

"She gets upset talking about Trace."

"I suppose so. Well, just between you and me, I think she'd been out looking for Trace after a big, ol' knock-down, drag-out fight," Patty whispered, although there was no one to hear. "She was upset that whole day. I felt bad for her. One look at her and you knew something big had happened. I think your mama knew he wouldn't be coming back."

RUBY CAME HOME LATE smelling of grease and cigarette smoke. McCall had been waiting for her. Her mother looked tired and there were blue lines on her calves from spending so many years on her feet.

McCall felt sorry for her mother and guilty. How different Ruby's life might have been if she hadn't gotten pregnant. Just as things could have been different if Trace had lived.

Or things could have turned out just the way they had.

"Didn't you work today?" her mother asked.

Had Ruby heard about her visit with Red Harper and thought McCall was checking up on her? "Nick had something come up and asked me to fill in for him."

Ruby glanced over at her as she entered her trailer, and McCall saw worry in her mother's eyes. All the questions about her father. The visit to her grandmother. Talking to Red about Trace. Now to find McCall waiting here for her. No wonder Ruby looked worried.

"I had a beer earlier with Red to talk to him about my father," McCall said as they entered the trailer, figuring Red had already warned Ruby. "You didn't tell me the two of you were going out."

Her mother shrugged. "It's just a date to a movie." She turned to look at her daughter and for a moment McCall thought her mother might cry. "Am I why you don't date?" Ruby asked, the question coming out of the blue.

She squirmed under her mother's intense gaze. "There's no one I want to go out with."

"There hasn't been anyone since that Crawford boy."

"I've been busy."

"Not *that* busy."

"Mom—"

"Fine. I know that boy broke your heart, but, McCall, it was years ago. You have to get back on the horse that bucked you off."

McCall laughed. That was exactly what her mother had been doing since her husband left her. "And how has that worked out for you? Have any of these men you dated made you forget my father?"

This time there was no doubt about the tears in her mother's eyes.

"I'm sorry. I—"

"No, you're right," Ruby said with a shake of her head. "I keep looking for what I had with Trace." She smiled ruefully as she swiped at her tears. "What else can I do, baby? At least the man you're in love with is still around and available. That should tell you something. If you weren't so stubborn—"

"You don't know anything about it."

"Don't I? I know what that boy did to you. He broke your heart. Just like your daddy broke mine." Her mother turned away and said, "You want some coffee?"

"No, thanks," McCall said as she watched her mother go into the kitchen to pour herself what was left of the coffee and reheat it in the microwave.

"Mom, I'm sorry, but I need to ask about my father."

"Fine, let's get this over with," Ruby said as she leaned against the counter and blew on her coffee to cool it. "Then I mean it, McCall, I don't want to hear any more about him, okay?"

McCall hated this, but she was afraid her mother might have found out about another woman and done something desperate, something she'd regretted all these years.

"All these years I've heard rumors, whispers behind

my back, about my father. Now I need to know the truth. Was there another woman?"

Ruby put down her coffee, angry now. "You heard Trace chased girls the way some dogs chase cars, right?"

"Is it true? Did he cheat on you?" McCall knew her mother. No way would Ruby have just taken that lying down, and after what Patty had told her, McCall didn't like what she'd been thinking.

Ruby made another swipe at the tears that brimmed in her lashes. "There was talk. Your father swore there was nothing going on."

"Going on with whom?"

Ruby shifted on her feet, wrapping her arms around herself again, her mouth pinched. "Geneva Cavanaugh. She'd dumped him to marry Russ Cherry before Trace and I got together. He took it hard. Then Russ got killed and Geneva disappeared, leaving behind her two babies."

"My father didn't run away with Geneva Cherry, Mom." She could see that this had been her mother's fear for the past twenty-seven years.

Ruby began to cry. "You don't know that. They both disappeared about the same time."

McCall thought about the single grave. Wouldn't the killer have buried them together? Maybe not. The pickup was still missing, and who knew what was inside it?

"Someone would have been heard from them by now if they'd run away together," she said, just for something to say.

Ruby shrugged.

"Was there anyone else?" McCall had to ask.

Her mother looked away. "Sandy."

"Sandy?"

"After Geneva, Trace was dating Sandy Thompson. That's when he and I got together."

"Sandy *Thompson* Sheridan?" The sheriff's wife? Her boss's wife? McCall stared at her mother. "You *stole* Trace from her?"

"I didn't *steal* him. You can't steal men like candy from a grocery store. I was in love with Trace. I'd always *loved* him."

"So all was fair in love and war," McCall quipped. Her mother never ceased to amaze her. This explained a lot, she realized. The cold shoulder Sandy had always given her.

Grant and Sandy had gotten married right after high school and gone away to college together. Grant became a lawyer, Sandy a homemaker. When they'd returned to Whitehorse, Grant became county attorney. Sandy had gotten involved in social activities.

McCall closed her eyes, seeing things too clearly. "You *seduced* him."

"Haven't you ever wanted anything more than life itself?"

McCall hated that Luke Crawford instantly came to mind.

"That was how I felt about your father. I would have done anything to be with him."

"Even get pregnant." McCall opened her eyes. Hadn't she long suspected this was the case?

Her mother's face fell. "Yes. Now you know the truth. I got pregnant to take him away from Sandy and force him to marry *me*."

So Pepper Winchester had been right.

Ruby was crying again. "I thought…" She stepped over to a chair and dropped into it, pulling her knees up to wrap her skinny arms around them, holding on as if for dear life. "I thought once we were a family, once you were born…" Her voice trailed off. She sniffed and McCall handed her a tissue from the box by the couch. "I guess I got what I deserved. The bad karma came back and bit me in the ass."

"You didn't deserve what you got," McCall said, fearing the killer might not agree. "Let me understand this. Trace and Sandy didn't break up until it came out about your pregnancy? How did Sandy take this news?"

Her mother mugged a face. "Sandy said Trace and I ruined her life but she seems to have survived just fine, lives in that big house up on the hill, married to the sheriff. Married him right after Trace broke up with her."

McCall frowned, unnerved by the timing. How hurt and angry had Sandy been? Hurt and angry enough to take it out on Trace?

"Mom, isn't it possible Sandy loved my father as much as you did?"

Ruby scoffed at that. "Trace was the love of my life. You haven't seen me marry anyone else, have you? It sure didn't take Sandy long to get over Trace, did it?"

Maybe that was because Trace was dead to her. Dead and buried.

Another thought struck McCall, one that sent a chill through her. Sandy had obviously married Grant on the rebound. He had to have realized that. Which brought up the question: how had Sheriff Grant Sheridan felt about Trace Winchester?

LUKE PARKED IN THE SHADOWS of the towering cotton-woods. As he got out, the breeze carried the scent of the new leaves that had just started coming out on the trees. They fluttered, making a sound like a whisper.

In the distance, a hawk let out a cry, and the forest paralleling the river fell silent. Twilight had settled into the cottonwoods. Through the thick bare branches, he could see the colors of the sunset deepening against the darkening sky.

It was early for poachers, but he'd noticed that this poaching ring seemed to be hitting at different times.

The quiet in the river bottom lulled him, his thoughts sneaking up on him as he walked along a fishing trail. There were times that he was at his most vulnerable, like now, and his thoughts turned to McCall.

She hadn't changed much from the girl he'd fallen in love with. If anything she was more beautiful. And headstrong and independent and prickly as a porcupine. She'd done just fine for herself without any help from anyone.

What was crazy was that he believed in his heart that they belonged together. If it wasn't for what had happened back when they were seniors in high school—

The sound of the rifle shot made him jump. The soft boom carried along the river bottom sending a flock of ducks rising up in a spray of water nearby.

He froze, listening, anticipating a second shot, hoping he would be able to determine which direction it had come from. The second shot came seconds later, followed by a quick third, then silence.

Luke took off running through the trees to where

he'd parked his pickup. From his estimation, the shots had come from a quarter mile downriver.

At his pickup, he jumped behind the wheel and took off down the road, knowing they would hear him coming.

By now at least one of them should be up to his elbows in blood from gutting out the deer they'd shot. They would hear his pickup engine and have to decide whether to load up the deer or just make a run for it.

Either way, he would have them if their tire treads matched the plaster casts he'd made of their last three kills.

The poachers were getting more brazen, killing one deer after another even though they must know he was tracking them. That kind of boldness often ended badly.

As he raced along the narrow windy dirt road that ran parallel to the river, Luke wished he'd taken the time to pull on his bulletproof vest. The men he was chasing would be armed.

As he came around a bend, he saw a pickup come barreling out of one of the many fishing access roads in a cloud of dust. All he was able to tell about the truck was that it was dark colored and an older model.

As Luke hit his lights and siren, he saw through the dust that one of the poachers was in the back of the truck—and the man wasn't alone.

The rising dust from the pickup made it impossible to ID the man, though—or get a license plate number on the fleeing vehicle.

As the truck took one of the tight, narrow curves too fast, Luke heard the screech of metal as a fender skinned one of the cottonwoods at the edge of the road. An instant later something large came tumbling out of the back of the truck.

Luke slammed on his brakes, skidding to a stop just inches from the carcass lying in the middle of the road.

For a heart-stopping moment, he'd thought the poacher had fallen out of the back of the pickup. But then he smelled the familiar scent of the animal's blood on the breeze—the dead deer blocking the road.

In the distance, the pickup disappeared over a rise as he watched, the poachers getting away. Again.

SANDY SHERIDAN LIVED WITH her husband, Grant, in a house up on the hill overlooking Whitehorse. The houses up here were newer. In Whitehorse, moving from the older homes to the hill was considered a step up in both lifestyle and status.

McCall parked in front of a split-level much like the others on the hill. She'd waited until the sheriff had left for a sheriffs' conference in Billings.

Even though it was late, Sandy Sheridan answered the door still wearing her robe and slippers, both white and fluffy. Her hair was sprayed into an updo that not even one of Whitehorse's stiff breezes could dislodge.

She'd applied fresh makeup, her cheeks looking flushed, eyes bright and ringed with mascara. McCall wondered what she was getting so duded up for at this time of the day. Or for whom.

"If you're looking for Grant, he's not here. He's at—"

"The Montana Sheriff's Association meeting in Billings. I know. Actually it's you I wanted to see," McCall said.

"Oh?" Sandy was her mother's age, early forties, but

the years had been kinder. "I guess I can spare a few minutes," she said, glancing at her watch, clearly annoyed as she stepped back to let McCall enter the house.

The house was furnished with pale furniture against white walls and drapes, giving the place a sterilized, cold feel.

"I'd offer you something to drink but—"

"I'm here about you and Trace Winchester," McCall said, cutting to the chase.

Sandy looked as if she'd just slammed her fingers in a car door. She opened her mouth but nothing came out. Earlier she'd been standing, looking impatient, now she lowered herself into a nearby off-white club chair.

"I beg your pardon?" she said.

"Oh, I'm sorry. I'd heard that you were in love with him, and I'm talking to people who knew my father."

Sandy let out a nervous laugh. "Why? That was high school."

"Some people never get over high school—or their first loves." As McCall knew only too well. "Look, I know you were dating my father when my mother got pregnant with me."

Sandy's face stiffened in anger belying her words. "That is ancient history. I really don't have the time to—"

"I should have known what I heard wasn't true. If you'd been that much in love with my father, you wouldn't have married Grant so quickly."

"I *loved* Trace," Sandy snapped, taking the bait. "We were going to get married, but then your mother…" She waved a hand through the air, hurriedly regaining her composure.

"You're *still* in love with my father," McCall said, unable to contain her shock. What was it about the man that made women love him so desperately even after everything he did to them?

Sandy looked away. "Don't be silly. That was—"

"Twenty-seven years ago. Not even time can change some things, though, huh."

"I really don't want to talk to you about this," she said, getting to her feet. "It isn't any of your business or your mother's."

Unfortunately, McCall feared it just might be. "You must have hated Trace for betraying you the way he did," she said as she rose to leave.

"I was angry. Who wouldn't be?"

"I think I would have wanted to kill him."

Sandy said nothing, her expression though said it all.

"I can see that he hurt you terribly. I'm sorry."

Tears filled the older woman's eyes. She brushed at them, obviously embarrassed and angry, and now her mascara was running.

"You've brought up a painful time in my life," Sandy said. "But that's all behind me. As you can see, I did quite well without Trace Winchester."

McCall stared at her, seeing a miserably unhappy woman behind the perfectly made-up face. "Yes, I can see that."

"Now if you don't mind…"

"What about Grant?" McCall asked, stopping at the door. "Does he know you never got over my father?"

Sandy opened the door. "Why are you asking about this after all these years? Does my husband know you're here?" She fumbled in the pocket of her robe for her cell phone.

"Don't worry, I'm leaving," McCall said, stepping past her. "I wouldn't want to make you late for your… *appointment*."

As she left, McCall glimpsed a car parked under a large old tree at the far end of the dead end street. Sandy hadn't needed to call her husband. He already knew about McCall's visit. Grant had apparently lied to both of them about going to the sheriffs' meeting.

But as McCall drove away, she wondered who Grant had been spying on—*her* or his wife.

LUKE LAY ON THE BED in his small camper trailer, unable to fall sleep. He'd planned to take a nap before staking out a spot on the river later tonight.

Through his bedroom window he could see the dark skeleton of his house and hear the breeze whispering through the beams as clouds scudded past in the gathering dusk.

He blamed McCall for his restlessness. The woman haunted his thoughts, making him ache with a need he hadn't been able to fill with any other woman. Had he thought the years would have changed McCall's mind about him? Or her feelings?

At times like this, he'd always turned to his work. He forced his thoughts to the poachers' pickup and how close he'd come to catching them earlier. He'd only gotten a glimpse of the truck as it came flying out of the fishing access, dust billowing.

The pickup was somewhere between brown and a rusted red. A good fifty years old. Something from the late fifties, early sixties. A beater. If he had to guess, he'd say a '62 Ford.

There were more than a few around in this part of the country. Hell, Buzz even used to own one.

Maybe he still did.

Luke sat up with a curse. He hadn't seen Buzz's old pickup for years. It used to be parked in the back of that old barn behind Buzz's lake house. Hell, it probably didn't even run anymore.

He swore again. He knew he wouldn't get any sleep if he didn't find out if that truck was still there. Buzz hadn't driven it in years. But that didn't mean someone else hadn't.

It was crazy. Or maybe not so crazy. He thought about that night years ago when he and Eugene had taken the pickup on a joyride. Buzz always kept the keys in the truck's ignition. Since the barn was a good distance from the lake house, they'd had no trouble taking out the pickup—and returning it—without Buzz being the wiser.

Luke had this crazy idea that someone might be using Buzz's pickup to poach deer. The irony didn't escape him. Nor would it have someone like Trace Winchester, who would have loved to rub it in Buzz's face.

Irony? Or payback?

It was dark by the time Luke parked on the road behind his uncle's old barn and killed the engine. He sat for a moment listening to the sounds of the night before he grabbed his flashlight and climbed out.

The moon was a sliver of white against the darkening sky. A few stars glittered through the veil of clouds. A breeze carried the distinct odors of the lake. Through the trees he could see the lake house. No vehicle parked next to it. Buzz wasn't home.

He breathed in the familiar scents, asking himself what the hell he was doing here about to creep around like a cat burglar.

But as he neared the old wooden structure he knew the reason he hadn't waited was that he didn't want Buzz to know. No reason to set his uncle off when Luke was probably wrong about the pickup being the one he'd seen the poachers driving.

He reached the back side of the barn before he turned on the flashlight. The lake house was on the opposite side. Even if Buzz happened to return, he wouldn't be able to see the light or hear anything from the house.

Luke slipped through the space between the two hinged barn doors. Dust motes danced in the flashlight beam that barely penetrated the dark, vast interior.

The barn still smelled of hay and manure even though it hadn't been used for either hay or livestock in years.

At a rustling sound, Luke swung around, leading with the beam of the flashlight. A cat scurried out the gap in the doors. As the dust and his heart settled back down, he probed the dark recesses of the barn with the paltry beam of the flashlight.

Luke shone the light into the dark corner where the '62 Ford pickup was always parked.

Empty.

He stared at the hole where the truck had been parked for so many years. He'd been wrong. Relief swept over him, letting him finally admit that he'd thought Eugene might have been using the old pickup.

But when had Buzz gotten rid of it? And maybe more important, whom had he sold it to?

As Luke ran the beam over the space where the truck

had been parked, he noticed the faint tire tracks in the dust. The pickup hadn't been gone that long. No, not that long at all, he thought as he squatted down to touch a dark spot on the dirt floor of the barn.

The spot where the pickup had recently dripped oil was still wet.

McCALL LEFT SANDY'S, surprised how dark it had gotten. Clouds skimmed just over the treetops, the limbs whipping in the wind.

The air was damp with the promise of rain and the growing darkness heavy and oppressive. Her headlights did little to hold back the night as she left the lights of Whitehorse in her rearview mirror and drove toward her cabin on the river.

She was tired, bone weary and sick at heart. She'd forced her mother to bare her soul and found out things about her father that she'd never wanted to know.

He's dead, McCall, why can't you just let it go?

Because she couldn't. Just as she couldn't get over Luke Crawford. She'd never believed in all that first love stuff that made good television movies. But Luke had been her first love, her only love.

Sometimes she thought about what her life would have been like if things had worked out for them. They could be married now, might even be parents.

She had a sudden image of Luke holding a baby and felt her eyes blur with tears. She rubbed them, telling herself she should be watching for deer along this stretch of narrow two-lane dirt road that wound through the large, old cottonwoods along the river, instead of bawling over what might have been.

But the night reminded her of another night ten years ago, the night she gave herself to Luke Crawford next to a small campfire beside the river. It had been the first time for both of them and so amazing that she'd known then no other man would make her feel the way Luke had.

That was the night he'd told her he loved her and wanted to marry her. She'd been so young and naive, she'd believed him, she thought now. And yet he'd been so tender, so loving—

As she came around a bend in the road, a vehicle came careening out of one of the fishing access roads. She saw the dust in her headlights an instant before she saw the vehicle.

The fool was driving without his headlights on.

She'd barely recognized that fact when the driver of the vehicle flashed on his headlights—and headed directly at her.

Chapter Seven

Luke couldn't shake his uneasy feeling as he left his uncle's barn and headed down the narrow, dirt river road. He caught glimpses of the moon through the tall cottonwoods. Clouds skimmed past overhead giving the night a surreal feel.

When he'd stopped by his uncle's cabin for a moment, he'd thought he heard the sound of a vehicle in the distance. Buzz hardly ventured anywhere other than town occasionally and then only during the day. It seemed strange that he wasn't home tonight.

Luke tried his uncle's cell phone. It went straight to voice mail. He didn't leave a message.

He'd waited for a few minutes, thinking Buzz would be home any minute, and then left, worried about what he'd discovered in the barn. He'd made a cast of the tire tracks but he hadn't needed to compare it with the other casts he'd taken from poaching sites. The distinct tracks in the dust had matched the ones from the poachers' vehicle. Someone was using Buzz's truck to poach deer, and Luke had a pretty good idea who that person was.

As for Eugene's accomplice, it could be any one of his lowlife friends.

As Luke rounded a curve in the road, he saw headlights at an odd angle. His heart thundered in his chest as he recognized the pickup in the ditch. McCall?

Pulling over, he grabbed his flashlight and jumped out. The pickup's front tires were on the road, headlights angled upward, the back tires buried in the dirt of the deep, narrow ditch.

From the dust still settling on the road, Luke guessed that the accident had just happened. All he could think was that it was a wonder she hadn't rolled the truck as he rushed to the driver's side and jerked open the door, the dome light coming on.

"McCall, are you—" He never got the words "all right" out.

She came out of the pickup swinging. He felt the sharp smack of her palm against the side of his face before he could restrain her.

"What in the hell?" he demanded as he looked into her eyes, saw the fear and the anger. But it was the fear that changed everything. He'd never seen her afraid before. He remembered the only other time he'd seen her vulnerable and, like now, she'd been in his arms.

She tried to take another swing, but he had her arms pinned down. Her mouth opened to say something, but her words were lost as his mouth dropped to hers. She struggled, but only for a moment.

He felt the fight go out of her as if, like him, she'd lost herself in the kiss—just the way she had all those years ago.

Then as if reason came back to her, she shoved him

away. She was breathing hard, and he couldn't tell if it was from the kiss or her earlier anger.

"You bastard," she said on a ragged breath.

"It was just a kiss, McCall." A lie. That powerful thing between them couldn't have been more evident. For those amazing moments, she'd been kissing him back, but that could have been enough to make her even angrier.

She advanced on him. He could still feel the sting of her slap and thought for a moment she would try to hit him again.

"You ran me off the road!"

He stared at her in the glow of the lights coming from their headlights and the dome light inside her open pickup door. "Whoa. I found you in the ditch. Are you saying someone purposely ran you off the road?"

She narrowed her gaze at him. "Not someone. *You.* If you think you can scare me away from investigating your uncle—"

"Are you crazy? You can't believe I would purposely try to run you off the road. Let alone that I would try to interfere in your investigation." He saw her expression. "Yeah, I guess you can. Why should you believe me? You've never believed anything I've ever told you. Not ten years ago. Not now. My mistake for thinking you needed my help."

She took a breath and let it out slowly before glancing down the dark road. "You didn't just come flying out of that fishing access site directly at me?"

He shook his head, too angry with her and himself to speak. Why the hell had he kissed her? He'd only managed to make things worse. But once he had her in his arms, he hadn't been able to help himself.

"Then where is the other pickup?" she demanded.

"I have no idea."

"I thought…" She stared at him as if really seeing him. "The headlights came right at me, I swerved and lost control and when I looked up…"

"There I was," he said.

"I'm sorry, I guess…"

If it had been anyone other than McCall, he might have thought the driver imagined another truck. Or had been unintentionally run off the road by someone.

But this was McCall.

"I saw dust as I came around the corner," he said, trying to remember the scene before he'd realized it was McCall's pickup and lost all reason. "I just assumed you'd made the dust when you crashed in the ditch."

"A pickup came right at me."

He felt himself start. "You saw that it was a pickup?"

"The headlights. They were high, so maybe I only got the *impression* it was a truck. Wait, no, I remember the way the back of the vehicle spun out as it turned onto the river road and came toward me. It was a pickup."

As Luke looked down the dark road, a sliver of fear burrowed under his skin. He doubted it was a coincidence that he'd been looking for a pickup, heard a vehicle as he was leaving Buzz's—and one had just run McCall off the road.

What worried him was the fear that the pickup—and McCall being run off the road—had something to do with not only Buzz's truck, but also his uncle.

McCALL HUGGED HERSELF against the cold Montana April night and the emotions Luke Crawford had set off like fireworks inside her.

He made her heart beat too fast, her pulse race, her body ache. He had when she was seventeen. He was even more desirable now, she thought, remembering the feel of his arms around her and the kiss. She reminded herself that this was the man who'd broken her heart, but that old bitterness didn't have the bite it used to.

"I'm sorry I accused you of running me off the road."

He was standing so close she could smell his woodsy male scent. She could see that her accusation had hurt more than the slap.

She hugged herself tighter at the memory of his arms around her, the solid, strong feel of his body, his mouth on hers. "And I'm sorry I hit you."

His gaze locked with hers. "I'm sorry I kissed you."

Damn the man. She wanted to smack him again.

"Yes, I'm sorry you did, too."

"I should get my tow rope," he said, clearly upset. "I think I can pull you out with my truck."

She nodded and felt something break inside her as he brushed past her, anger in every line of his body. "Thanks," she said.

He mumbled something under his breath she couldn't hear as he headed for his truck.

McCall leaned against the cold metal of her pickup and stared at his broad back silhouetted against his headlights. How could she have thought he would want to hurt her? Because he'd hurt her before.

She took a deep breath of the cold night air and, touching her finger to her lips, felt her traitorous heart quicken at the memory of the kiss.

His kiss had brought back the past in one fell swoop. That night beside the campfire, the stars glittering overhead, the night she'd been seventeen and so wonderfully in love.

Her skin ached at the memory of their lovemaking beside the campfire.

"McCall? You ready?"

Lost in the past, she started at the sound of his voice. Hurriedly, she climbed back behind the wheel and slammed her pickup door.

With a jolt, she realized that she'd been so shaken earlier she hadn't bothered to turn off the engine. Her hands trembled as she was reminded of the near head-on collision before she'd swerved and lost control, ending up in the ditch.

It could have been so much worse.

She saw that Luke had turned his truck around, hooked up the tow rope and was just waiting for her to give him a signal that she was ready.

She whirred down her window. "Ready when you are."

He gave her a thumbs-up before disappearing into the cab of his truck. She waited as he pulled forward, the tow rope tightening until she felt the tension stretch between them.

All these years of being apart and now they'd been thrown together how many times in the past two days? If she believed in fate…

When she felt the tow rope grow taut, she gave her truck some gas. She could hear the dirt and gravel scrape against the undercarriage, then she was hauled up and out of the ditch and onto the road, forced to hit her brakes to keep from running into the back of Luke's pickup.

Putting the truck in Park, she got out and stood between their two rigs as he unhooked the tow rope, trying not to notice the way the fabric of his shirt stretched over the hard muscles of his shoulders. "About earlier—"

"Forget it," he said, rising to his feet with the tow rope coiled in his hands.

If only she could forget.

"If you remember anything about the truck that ran you off the road…"

"Sure," she said, although she knew that wasn't going to happen. All she'd seen was dust, then bright headlights.

"I'm glad you're all right."

Both feet firmly planted on the ground. That was her.

He turned and started toward his pickup, all broad shoulders, long legs, slim hips and cowboy boots. But it was the way he moved, a long, lanky swagger…

"Luke?"

He stopped and looked back at her, waiting though wary.

"Nothing," she said. "Just…thanks."

He nodded, climbed into his pickup and drove away, leaving her wanting to pound her head against the side of her truck.

LUKE KNEW HE HAD TO BE dreaming because McCall lay next to him on the bed in his new house—the one he hadn't finished building, let alone moved into.

She was in his arms, her body warm and silky soft, scented with the sweet smells of summer. Her limbs were lightly suntanned, a sprinkling of freckles along the tops of her shoulders and the bridge of her nose.

He drew her closer, breathing her in, amazed that he hadn't lost her. He didn't question how it was that she was here with him. All those years apart seemed to melt away and he knew in his heart that this was where McCall was destined to be—with him.

Something jarred him. He closed his eyes tighter, fighting whatever was trying to pull him from the dream, knowing that the moment he came fully awake, McCall would be gone. Gone, just as she had been for the past ten years. Only this time, lost to him forever.

The ringing of his cell phone dragged him up from the dream. He stirred, still keeping his eyes closed, still fighting that moment when he would know for certain it had all just been a dream.

The phone rang again. Luke cursed and opened his eyes. The bed next to him was cold and empty.

He rolled over and snatched up the phone. "Luke Crawford." His gaze went to the lighted clock next to his bed—3:00 a.m.

And he knew even before he heard the rancher's voice that the poachers had hit again.

McCall woke before dawn. She blamed Luke Crawford for another fitful night. Showered and dressed, too antsy to sit around, she went out to examine her pickup to make sure there was no real damage.

The rear bumper was dented and filled with dirt and grass from the ditch, but apparently no real damage. With a shudder she remembered seeing the huge cottonwood trees that lined the road, fearing she couldn't get control of the pickup before plowing into them.

She was just thankful she had only ended up in the ditch. No harm done.

If only she could say as much for Luke's kiss. Damn him.

Desperately needing to get him off her mind, she got

in her pickup and drove south on Highway 191. It wasn't until she'd gone a few miles that she realized she'd be driving right past his house.

She'd heard he'd bought the old Crawford place that had belonged to his parents before their deaths. Buzz had sold it to an out-of-state corporation when he took Luke in.

But when Luke had returned to town, he'd somehow been able to buy it back. She'd heard he was living in a camp trailer on the property while he built a house.

At this early hour, she was tempted to drive down to his trailer and wake him up. If she couldn't get any rest, it didn't seem fair that he should. As the saying went, misery loves company.

But she had no desire to see him. Especially after their encounter last night.

Clouds low, rain threatening, she drove another few miles before she turned off on the road that led to the ridge where she'd found her father's grave.

A cold wind rocked the patrol SUV as she sat staring at the muddy grave—and a dozen footprints around it. She'd known this would happen once Rocky told people about it. Grave robbers had scoured the area looking for curios or clues to go with their theories on whose body had been buried there.

McCall told herself it would have been worse if she'd told the sheriff about the hunting license and cordoned off the grave with crime scene tape. Everyone in town would have had to come out and see for themselves. She had to be content with the fact that she'd gotten any evidence there was and turned it all in to the lab.

Except for the hunting license.

Taking her binoculars, she climbed out and walked along the spine of the ridge. It worried her what her mother had said about Geneva Cherry disappearing about the same time as Trace.

As she walked, she looked for signs of another grave but saw no place to bury another body. The ridge was rocky except for the area where her father had been buried.

So if Geneva had been with Trace that day and someone had gotten rid of them both, the killer hadn't buried them both here. Why bury one and not the other? Because Geneva's disappearance and Trace's weren't related? Unless Geneva had been the killer.

McCall walked out to where the ridge narrowed to a windy point. She raised her binoculars, wondering if her father had stood on this very spot looking through his rifle scope for antelope on opening day of the season.

As the Winchester Ranch came into view, McCall realized with a start that he could have been watching the house, could have maybe even seen people inside that morning.

Today the old lodge looked dark and cold under the cloak of clouds, lifeless behind the blank windows and weathered shutters.

A tumbleweed blew past on a gust, the wind howling around her, as McCall lowered her binoculars and wondered where a person might get rid of a large black Chevy pickup.

Sage- and pine-studded ridges ran out to rocky points as the land fell for miles toward the Missouri River. All those ravines. Wasn't it possible the pickup had been dumped in one? As wild as this country was it could have gone unnoticed for years.

But not twenty-seven years. Someone would have spotted it from the air or a hunter would have stumbled across it. Trace Winchester's pickup would have been known around the county—just as his antics were.

Where then? Where could you hide a vehicle so that it would never be found? She scanned the remote countryside, turning slowly in a circle, studying this unforgiving landscape.

Had the killer lured Trace out here, planning to kill him? Or had Trace's death been impulsive? Possibly even an accident? If it had been a hunting accident, why wouldn't the shooter have reported it—instead of burying the body and disposing of the pickup and rifle?

The ridge was far enough from Highway 191 that the killer wouldn't have been seen while burying the body. No need to hurry and yet the killer hadn't taken the time to dig a very deep grave. Nor had the killer taken the time to move the body to a better burial site.

Neither indicated premeditation.

So after digging a shallow grave and burying the body, then what?

Her father hadn't been out here alone. But had the killer ridden out here with him in his pickup? Or had the killer met him here? Either way, the killer needed to dispose of Trace's pickup quickly since it was so recognizable.

He would have probably gotten rid of the pickup, then come back and gotten his own rig as long as he didn't have to take the pickup far. He couldn't chance someone seeing Trace's truck, and since the only way out of here was Highway 191—

In the distance, McCall spotted something that made her pulse jump. Water the color of rust.

She focused the binoculars on the spot, her heart pounding as she saw a stock pond. Not just a stock pond, but one visible from her father's grave. The killer could have seen it or even known it was there.

How much water would it take to hide a pickup? Eight feet minimum, she estimated. As she started to lower the binoculars a windmill caught her eye and past it, a set of corrals.

She felt light-headed as she realized whose place she was looking at. The old Crawford ranch, where Luke Crawford was now building his house.

Over the wind and her thundering heart, McCall didn't hear the vehicle pull in. Nor did she hear someone approach from behind her until she felt the hand drop to her shoulder.

Chapter Eight

McCall jumped, startled. She spun around, her hand going to her holster, stopping short of her weapon as she recognized the man now standing on the lone ridge with her.

"I thought I might find you out here," Sheriff Grant Sheridan said, raising his voice to be heard over the wind. Frown lines deepened the furrows between his brows as the first drops of rain splashed down, hard and cold. "Let's talk in my rig."

McCall followed him back through the rain to his patrol SUV parked next to her pickup and climbed in, wondering how he'd known she'd be here, let alone why he'd driven way out here to look for her.

"What's up?" she asked, shaking raindrops off as she settled into the seat.

He started the engine, turning on the wipers and the heater. Rain pounded the roof and pinged off the hood.

"You tell me," he said as he looked past the rain and the rhythmic slap of the wipers toward the ridge. The rain slanted down in angry slashes, pelting the puddles already forming in the mud in front of the SUV. Fortunately the road back to the highway was rocky or they might have trouble getting out of here.

"I didn't realize you could see the Winchester Ranch from here," he said finally and glanced pointedly at the binoculars on the strap around her neck.

McCall followed his gaze to the ranch in the distance, but said nothing, her apprehension growing. Was this about Pepper Winchester?

That could explain why Grant looked worried. "Is there anything you want to tell me?" he asked.

"You mean, what I'm doing out here?" she asked, going on the defensive, fearing what had brought him all this way. "I wanted to check the site before my shift. Just as I figured, some locals have been out here digging around."

"But there wasn't anything to find, right?"

"I did a thorough search of the area the first time," she said, afraid of where this was going. "If there was anything to find, I found it."

The sheriff sighed. "McCall," he said his voice softening. "I got a call from the crime lab this morning."

She closed her eyes, surprised she was fighting tears even though she knew what the results of the DNA test were going to prove. She'd known the moment she'd found her father's hunting license in the muddy grave.

She heard the rustle of papers and opened her eyes to look over at him. He had his head down and she saw the faxed report now lying on his lap.

The patrol SUV suddenly felt too small. She lowered her window a few inches even though the cold rain blew in soaking one side of her to the skin.

"According to the report, the bones are from a male in his early twenties," Grant said without looking at her. "The lab estimates the body has been in the ground for the past twenty-five to thirty years. But I would imagine none of this comes as a surprise to you, does it."

"What about the DNA?" McCall asked, her voice breaking. "Was it a match?"

His gaze softened as he looked over at her and nodded. "I'm sorry."

Her eyes burned.

Grant cleared his throat. "I can't imagine that this was just a hunch on your part. How did you know?"

"I found my father's hunting license where the body had been buried before the rainstorm washed the remains down into the gully," she said quietly. "The license was still in the orange plastic case."

"You knew it was a probable murder scene and yet—"

"I documented everything I found with photos," she said quickly. "I treated it as a murder scene."

"You withheld evidence."

"I couldn't be sure until the DNA report came back."

He was shaking his head, clearly angry and disappointed in her. "You're my first female deputy. Do you realize how hard I had to fight to get you on the force?"

She could imagine. "I appreciate that. But he was my father, I had—"

"You're a deputy first and foremost. The moment you found this you should have roped off the crime scene, you should have come to me—"

"I bagged everything at the scene and photographed it. I knew once Rocky got back to town and started talking every looky-loo would be out here—especially if I'd roped it off with crime scene tape, and I couldn't be sure until I got the DNA report back." She took a breath. "And I knew that the minute I turned that hunting license over to you that you'd pull me off the case."

"Pull you off the case? Hell, I have no choice but to suspend you, McCall. You're lucky I don't fire you on the spot."

"I understand." She reached for her gun and badge.

He studied her as she handed over both, then pulled the hunting license in the orange plastic case from her pocket and gave him that, as well.

It was hard to give up the license, but she'd made two copies of it, knowing this day was coming. Those were hidden in her pickup.

The sheriff shook his head as he dropped the license into an evidence bag. "You destroyed any fingerprints on the license."

"The killer didn't touch it. If he had, he would have taken it along with Trace's wallet, his boots, his truck and anything else that made identifying the body possible twenty-seven years ago."

Grant didn't look any happier to hear that. "I heard you'd been asking questions around town about your father."

Had Sandy told him? Somehow McCall doubted that. But he must have wondered what McCall had been doing at his house that day.

"When I saw you headed out this direction this morning, I just had a feeling…" he said now. "I thought it had to do with the Winchesters but I never imagined…"

"My father didn't leave town," McCall said, her voice breaking. "Someone killed him and buried him out there." She pointed at the cloud-cloaked ridge. "For twenty-seven years, he was there and someone knew he was there."

"Anything else you've withheld from me?" Grant asked.

She shook her head and watched as he folded the report and put it into the breast pocket of his coat before looking over at her again.

"You have already compromised this investigation. If you care about your job, you'll take your two-week suspension and do nothing else to jeopardize your position with my department. In the meantime, this is a crime scene and you're officially suspended and off the case. Is that understood?"

"Yes." She opened her door and stepped out into the rain. The sheriff did the same, bringing with him a large roll of yellow tape and a handful of wooden stakes.

He didn't look at her as he began to cordon off the crime scene twenty-seven years too late.

Buzz CLEARLY HAD SOMETHING on his mind when he finally answered his cell phone. "What's up?" he asked, sounding impatient.

"Did I catch you in the middle of something?" Luke asked.

"No, I'm just on my way to Billings so I might lose cell phone service at any time. What's going on?"

"Billings?" Luke said, forgetting for a moment his real reason for calling his uncle.

"Eugene and I are going down to talk to the guy he owes the money to, see if we can work something out."

So Eugene was with him. "You sure that's a good

idea?" Luke regretted the words the moment they were out. *None of your business.* He mentally kicked himself as he heard the anger in Buzz's voice.

"Compared to the alternative?" his uncle demanded. "Or we could just let him get what's coming to him. Is that your plan?"

Luke didn't have a plan. Nor did he think he should be expected to. He held his tongue, trying not to let Buzz tick him off any more than he just had.

"I was calling to ask you about that old pickup you keep in your barn," he said, anxious to find out what he wanted and get off the line.

"What about it?"

"I guess I'm surprised you still have it."

"It's not worth getting rid of. Why do you care?"

"Does it still run?"

"It did last time I drove it." His uncle's irritation wasn't lost even though the line was filling with static. "Is there something you wanted?"

"We can talk when you get back. When is that?"

"Tomorrow. Listen, I'm losing you. I gotta go." And with that his uncle was gone.

Luke snapped his phone shut, worried about Buzz and Eugene going to Billings given the people they would be meeting with. Even more worried about Buzz's old pickup that should have been in the barn last night when McCall was being run off the road.

As dusk settled over the Missouri River Breaks, Luke thought about going to Billings, telling himself he needed to know the truth and it couldn't wait until Buzz and Eugene got back.

He tried his uncle's cell again to find out where they

would be staying only to get voice mail. He'd have to wait until they returned to Whitehorse.

He'd spent most of the day checking fishing licenses and tags down on the Missouri. Now, headed home, Highway 191 rose up out of the river bottom to trail along the high ridges. From here he could see how the land had eroded into deep gullies and ravines as it fell to the river.

Climbing out of the Breaks, the highway skirted the Little Rockies, the pines shimmering in the sunlight. As the land opened up into rolling prairie dotted with sage and antelope, Luke usually felt a sense of peace.

Today though, he couldn't shake the bad feeling that seemed to follow him like a threatening thunderhead. He didn't know if this sense of foreboding had to do with his cousin's gambling or the poaching and pickup.

He drove past the turnoff to his place and through Whitehorse on out to Nelson Reservoir. This time he didn't need to sneak so he drove right up to his uncle's barn.

A wall of hot air hit him as he got out of his pickup, surprised at how hot the day must have gotten up here compared to down on the Missouri River.

This time, the moment he stepped into the barn, he cut his flashlight beam to the spot where the pickup should have been.

And was.

The rusted red truck sat in the spot Luke remembered it residing for years. He felt the hood. Cold. When had it been returned? he wondered as he opened the driver's side door and glanced inside.

The keys were in the ignition—just as they always were. He shone his flashlight across the bench seat, then onto the floorboards.

Mud. A large piece not quite dry. He looked closer, hoping to find a boot print he could use. No such luck.

He searched the rest of the pickup, finding nothing unusual, then closed the door and turned the flashlight beam on the tires. By now he knew the tread of his poachers' rig by heart. They had matched the tread in the dust where this truck had been parked before it was returned. All he needed was—

Luke frowned. To his surprise, the treads on these tires *didn't* match those taken at the poaching sites. Someone had changed the tires.

He moved along the side to the truck bed. It had recently been washed out. A red flag since the rest of the pickup hadn't been washed.

Had Buzz used the truck for something? The bad feeling he'd had earlier intensified as he ran a finger along the edge of the tailgate, his finger coming away tinted red.

Blood.

McCALL DIDN'T WANT her grandmother or her mother finding out about Trace before she could tell them herself.

She'd crawled out on a limb when she'd withheld evidence from the sheriff. Now she was about to saw that limb off. But in her heart, she knew what she had to do. She knew the sheriff would wait until he had another DNA sample and report before he'd go to either Ruby or Pepper about the bones found on the ridge.

It wouldn't be enough that McCall's DNA had matched because her parentage was considered questionable. Just as it probably wouldn't be enough proof for her grandmother.

As she drove toward the Winchester Ranch for the second time within days, McCall didn't let that bother her. She owed her father this, she told herself as the green landscape rolled past.

The sky was clear, the day warm for this time of year in this part of Montana. She loved spring. It had been a long, cold winter, but this was her home, country she loved, land that she knew.

She put down her window, letting the fresh air blow in and told herself her grandmother would see her. Enid wouldn't be able to stop her.

The nice thing about the Winchester Ranch being so far from civilization was that even if her grandmother called the sheriff, by the time he got to the ranch McCall would be gone. Of course, if Grant was determined to arrest her, he would know where to find her.

She smiled, realizing she might be more like her father than she wanted to admit.

As she turned into the ranch yard, she saw a curtain move on the second floor and the old dog came out barking and growling. *Well, they know I'm here, anyway.*

She got out of the pickup, no longer fearful of the dog. Her grandmother really should get a meaner, younger dog if she was serious about keeping people away.

She didn't even get to knock before the door was flung open. Enid, looking like an ugly old bulldog, stood blocking the doorway, her lip curled in a snarl.

"Mrs. Winchester—"

"Will see me," McCall said cutting her off. "Tell her I have news about Trace." It surprised McCall how angry she was. Her mother said she'd inherited her father's temper, and he had apparently inherited it from his mother—if the fury McCall saw in her grandmother's face was any indication when she appeared.

"You were warned not to—"

McCall waved the copy of Trace's hunting license she'd brought her grandmother. "Do you want to know what happened to your son or not?"

Pepper Winchester stopped in midsentence. Enid offered to call the sheriff and was headed for the phone when Pepper stopped her. "Leave us alone."

Enid looked as if she were going to argue. Instead, she left in a huff, clearly furious at being sent away like hired help. McCall had to wonder again about the woman's relationship with her grandmother.

"If this is some kind of ruse to—"

"The sheriff hasn't called you?"

Pepper's hand went to her throat. "Why would Sheriff Sheridan—"

"My father never left town." She glanced past her grandmother and saw Enid lurking down the hallway, eavesdropping. "Is there somewhere we can talk in private?"

Pepper had gone very pale. McCall had the feeling that her grandmother had been expecting this visit from her, had known after McCall's last one that something other than curiosity had brought her here.

This time her grandmother led her into a small office. It appeared it hadn't been used in years, like most of the rest of the massive lodge.

Pepper closed the door but continued standing. "What is this about my son not leaving town?"

"A man named Rocky Harrison found some bones,"

McCall said, talking quickly, knowing any minute her grandmother could send her packing. "The bones had been washed from a shallow grave on a ridge." She stepped to the window and pushed back the curtain. "*That* ridge."

Her grandmother moved to stand by her, staring out at the ridge in the distance.

"This is a copy of what I found where those bones had been buried." McCall handed her the copies of the hunting license and the antelope tag. "The license and tag were protected because they were still in the plastic folder he carried them in."

Pepper's hands trembled as she took the pages and looked at the printing on them. She seemed to sway, but when McCall reached toward her, she quickly straightened.

"The bones can't be my son's," her grandmother said, her voice breaking. "You've made this up as an excuse to—"

"I had a DNA test run on the bones."

Pepper's gaze narrowed. "Comparing them to whose DNA?"

"Mine. The remains in that grave were my father's and assuming you're through denying I'm Trace Winchester's daughter…"

Her grandmother stared at her for a long moment before she moved like a sleepwalker over to one the leather chairs and sat down heavily. She motioned impatiently for McCall to sit, as well.

"Why hasn't the sheriff called me about this?"

"He will be calling you to request a sample of your DNA to run a comparison test," McCall said.

"These bones—"

"Were buried in a shallow grave on the ridge. The rainstorm the other night washed them down into a gully. The hunting license was buried in the mud in the grave."

Her grandmother's hand holding the copy of the license began to tremble again. She quickly stilled it. "You're telling me that someone killed my son."

McCall nodded. "Twenty-seven years ago."

"Who?"

McCall shook her head. "It will be next to impossible to find his killer after all this time."

Her grandmother bristled at that. "I'm sure the sheriff—"

"Grant Sheridan will turn the case over to the state crime lab but with a case this cold…"

Pepper recoiled with a shudder. "If you're saying I'll never know who killed my son… Trace will get justice if it takes my last dying breath."

She'd hoped that would be her grandmother's attitude. "Then help me find his killer."

"You?" Pepper scoffed at that. "You're a *deputy*. And you haven't even been one that long."

McCall had only a moment to wonder how her grandmother had known that.

Pepper shook her head and pushed herself to her feet. "I will hire the best private investigator that money can buy."

"And you will be wasting your money."

Her grandmother's eyes widened in surprise.

"You know the people in this part of the state," McCall said quickly. "You think anyone will talk to an outsider? People up here, even if they weren't all related, are close-knit. They're even suspicious of other Montanans let alone someone from out of state. Good luck with that."

"You are certainly a brash young woman."

Like my grandmother. "I intend to find out who killed my father no matter what the sheriff or the crime lab does or doesn't do," McCall said. "But I need your help. I need to know what my father was involved in twenty-seven years ago."

Her grandmother was shaking her head.

McCall rushed on. "I might be the only person who can find out the truth. Don't you see that? I'm a local, I have some training and he was *my* father."

"What makes you think anyone will talk to you?"

McCall smiled. "I'm the black sheep of the Winchesters. Everyone feels sorry for me because I've been treated so badly by my own grandmother."

The dagger found its mark. Her grandmother looked ashamed, but only for a moment. "You seem to have done fine without me."

"I need to know everything about my father—no matter what it is," McCall continued. "Are you willing to help me or not?"

"Why don't you ask your mother?"

McCall didn't even bother to answer that. "Are we going to keep pretending that I'm not Trace Winchester's daughter?"

Her grandmother moved to the window to gaze out in the direction of the wind-scoured ridge again. "I've just found out that my son is not only dead but that he was murdered and buried within sight of my ranch."

She turned to look at McCall, her eyes shiny with

unshed tears. "I'm not up to satisfying your curiosity about him right now."

"I'm sorry I had to bring you this news," McCall said. "But I knew you'd want to know right away."

Something softened in her grandmother's face, letting her grief show through.

"Are you sure you're all right?" McCall asked.

Her grandmother straightened, that moment of vulnerability gone. "You needn't concern yourself with me."

McCall nodded. "Let me know when you're ready to help me." She felt sorry for her grandmother as she left and wondered if she'd ever hear from her again. Doubtful. She was on her own finding her father's killer.

As she climbed into her pickup, she didn't see Enid, although she suspected the woman wasn't far away.

Driving away, McCall turned her thoughts to her mother and realized she had no idea how Ruby would take the news about Trace's murder.

Chapter Nine

On the way back to Whitehorse, McCall called the café. Her mother was scheduled to work a double shift. "Is Ruby still there?"

"She just stepped outside to sneak a cigarette," Leo, the cook, told her. "It's slow, so I think she's going to leave early. You want me to give her a message?"

"No, that's all right. I'll catch her," McCall said, and hung up as she came over the rise and saw the Milk River Valley—the town of Whitehorse at the heart of it.

As she drove into town, she spotted the small figure of her mother coming down the street from the café toward her vehicle. McCall swung to the curb and reached over to open the passenger side door.

Ruby leaned her head in through the open doorway. "Hop in."

Her mother looked startled but didn't argue as she slid into the seat and slammed the door. "Shouldn't you be working?"

McCall had figured by now it would be all over town about her getting suspended.

She drove out of town headed north just because that

was the way she was pointed. Out of the corner of her eye, she saw Ruby glance out the window then shoot her a questioning look.

"I got suspended for two weeks. I'll probably get fired." She looked over at her mother. "I withheld some evidence."

"You must have had your reasons. I'm sure if you talk to Grant—"

Something in the way her mother said the sheriff's first name… "That's right. You used to date Grant."

Ruby swore. "If this is why you picked me up, then just let me out now. I'm in no mood to have you give me crap about my love life or quiz me about your father." Her mother reached for her door handle. "I'm serious. Just let me out."

McCall glanced over at her mother. There was no good way to say this. "Trace didn't leave you. He never left Whitehorse at all."

"What are you talking about?" Ruby snapped. "Of course Trace left town. I wasn't serious about his mother hiding him all these years. Unless she locked him up in one of those rooms at the ranch."

"You heard Rocky found some bones south of town? They've been identified." She could feel her mother freeze. "Trace didn't leave you. He's been out there all these years."

Pepper hadn't been up there in twenty-seven years. Small spaces terrified her, and she wished she felt up to climbing the ladder to the third floor room instead of being forced to take the old elevator.

No one had been in this wing in years judging by the footprints she was leaving in the dust. This was the only other access and the walk here had worn her out. After McCall left, she'd retrieved her cane, hating that she needed it.

She stopped in the dark hallway. Years ago the light bulbs must have burned out. Only faint shafts of light cut through the shuttered windows as she touched the secret panel on the wall to reveal the old elevator.

The metal was cold as she pulled back the gate. Something skittered away in the elevator shaft making her shudder. She hesitated, then stepped into the tiny, cramped space, telling herself she should be more worried about the elevator's working condition than her claustrophobia.

As a newlywed, she hadn't understood the purpose of the room or why she had been told it and the elevator were off-limits to all but her husband, Call. She would later understand only too well.

The elevator smelled just as Trace's room had, old and musty, filled with ghosts from the past. As she closed the gate, she was bombarded by a barrage of memories that made her sick to her stomach.

Her breath came in gasps, her fingers trembling. She pushed the button that would take her up to the locked room.

"Pepper, why would you want to go up there again?" asked the voice in her head, a voice that sounded exactly like her husband, Call's. "What if you get trapped up there and no one finds you until the house is torn down or just falls down someday?"

Enid and Alfred were in the far wing of the house. They wouldn't have heard the elevator. Nor would they hear her cries for help. Eventually they would find her but by then—

The elevator groaned and clanked and for a moment she thought it wouldn't rise. Then with a jerk it began to ascend.

She pressed the hand holding the cane against the wall to steady herself, the other to her mouth to keep from crying out as the elevator inched upward.

In the small, isolated space she thought she could hear voices trapped from all those years ago. The screams of her children. The incessant crying and pleading. The empty finality when the elevator stopped.

Pepper reached for the metal gate, terrified the elevator might suddenly drop as she took a step out. Miraculously it didn't move as she stepped off to find herself standing at the edge of the small room.

The room was soundproof. Not even the bulletproof window opened. Anyone sent here could not be heard outside these walls. Nor seen through the one-way glass.

The only openings were small. Just large enough for a gun barrel to fit through.

"Why in God's name did you have this room built?" Pepper had demanded when Call had once caught her snooping. She'd been pregnant with their oldest child, Virginia, at the time.

Call had been furious with her. "It's for protection."

"Against whom?"

He'd only shaken his head and escorted her from the room.

It wasn't until later that she and her children learned that the room was also for punishment.

This room was where Call had locked her the day she'd tried to leave him.

RUBY BEGAN TO CRY QUIETLY. McCall wondered what her mother was thinking, what she was feeling. Was she relieved? Angry? Or just saddened by the news? McCall couldn't tell.

Ruby hid so much. Her only passion seemed to be men. It was the only time she let her emotions out. Over men she cried, swore, broke things, poured out her soul.

Except when it came to Trace Winchester. Maybe he really had been the love of her life, just as she claimed.

McCall turned off on the road to Sleeping Buffalo Resort and drove down to the hot springs, parking in front of the bar.

"I thought you might need a drink," she said to her mother.

Ruby wiped her eyes and opened her purse to pull out a wad of ones. "I'll buy if you'll go in and get us something."

McCall wasn't much of a drinker. "What do you want?"

"Tequila. Get a pint and something to chase it, okay?"

Tequila was the booze of preference for Ruby after a breakup. It seemed appropriate given the circumstances.

McCall took the wad of ones and got out. As she closed the pickup door, she saw her mother roll down her window and light a cigarette, her fingers trembling.

When she returned with a quart of orange juice, a pint of tequila and two paper cups, her mother stubbed out her cigarette. The pickup smelled of smoke and grease and sweat.

McCall handed everything to her mother and drove down by the lake, parking in the shade of a large old cottonwood.

Ruby busied herself making them both a drink. They touched cups, eyes meeting for a moment. McCall felt the impact finally.

Her father was dead. Murdered. Nothing would ever be the same. Especially if it turned out that Ruby had killed him.

Pepper started to step farther into the room when she was startled by movement. Something small fluttered in the far corner, making her stumble back. As she tried to still her racing pulse, she realized that the slight breeze coming up through the elevator shaft had rustled the small paper objects in the corner.

Frowning, she stepped closer. Paper party hats? They were faded with the years, but still recognizable as the tiny ones she'd purchased for Trace's birthday party. She'd bought the tiny ones for the grandchildren and had been upset when she'd seen them wearing them long before the party.

She remembered yelling at the bunch of them to get out of the house. They had scampered away.

She stared at the paper hats discarded like trash on the floor of the room, realization making her weak. They'd been in this room that they'd been forbidden to enter.

Pepper felt her anger rise as she counted the hats. Five? Had there been five children in here that day? She remembered how noisy they'd been, her two grandsons,

Cordell and Cyrus, and the nanny's boy, Jack. Had they taken extra hats or had someone been with them? She hadn't invited any other children. But that didn't mean that those two horrible neighboring ranch girls hadn't sneaked over.

As she started to rise, she saw something that stopped her heart stone-cold still before it took off like a wild horse.

What she'd first thought were cracks in the plastered wall, she now saw were words. Tiny, scrawled words scratched into the walls. They were everywhere—within child height.

Pepper closed her eyes unable to bear reading what her children had written up here while imprisoned in this horrible room.

The room had always been empty. No furniture. "It's no punishment if you fill the room full of toys or make it comfortable," Call had said.

When she'd tried to stop Call from using this room to punish their children, he'd told her he'd raise them his way, the way he'd been raised. "It's like breaking a horse. If you can't stand to watch, don't."

She couldn't stand to watch so she'd stood by help-lessly for years, she thought with a shudder.

That was until Trace had come along and she'd sworn Call wasn't "breaking" this one. Trace was seven when she'd decided to leave Call, taking her youngest son and fleeing.

Call had caught her and locked her in this room for three days.

Not long after that, her husband had gone off for a horseback ride and was never seen again.

She hadn't been able to save the others. As she opened her eyes again, she felt faint and thought she might have to sit down. She grabbed hold of the windowsill and looked out at the ridge in the distance where her son's body had been buried all those years. The same spot where he'd died?

This is why she'd had to come up here. She had to know if she could see the ridge from this room.

But now she saw that it would have been impossible to see what had happened on that far ridge at this distance. She'd been foolish to think there might have been an eyewitness, someone in the family who had inadvertently seen Trace's murder.

Suddenly the full weight of her loss hit her. She felt her knees give way, and even the cane couldn't support her as she dropped to the floor.

She lay there for a few minutes, letting the dam of tears burst and fall. She wept as she had the time she'd been locked in this room and cursed her son's killer.

Finally the tears subsided. She sat up feeling dizzy and light-headed. She shuddered at the thought that she was so weak or that the past was so strong.

As she started to get to her feet, anxious to leave this horrible room and the memories within these walls, she saw a small hole behind the window ledge. Someone had dug out the chinking from between the logs and made a space just large enough apparently to hide something.

In this case, a small pair of binoculars.

With a start she worked the binoculars from the hole, wiping them free of dust with her sleeve before raising them to look out at the ridge.

Her heart caught in her throat. She fought to keep down her lunch. She could see the ridge clearly right down to the crime scene tape flapping in the wind around her son's grave.

"To Trace," Ruby said and took a drink.

To you, Dad. McCall felt the kick of the tequila. She looked out at the sky-mirrored water. From here she could barely make out Buzz Crawford's house across the lake.

"I suppose by the time we get back to town everyone will know," Ruby said as she made herself another drink.

"Count on it." This was the biggest news to hit town in some time. "Are you going to be all right?"

Ruby laughed. "Hell, yes. The bastard didn't leave me." She laughed again and lifted her glass before downing half of it. "He might have stayed, you know. Things could have been different."

She nodded. Or they might have ended the same. They would never know.

But McCall liked to think her mother and father would have made it work and stayed together. She tried to imagine having a normal family. Whatever normal was.

As it was, history would have to be rewritten. Twenty-seven years of stories based on one false assumption. McCall thought of all the whispered rumors she'd heard about her father over the years.

Trace Winchester hadn't run out on them. True, he probably would have, given what McCall had learned about him and her mother. But he hadn't and that's what counted.

A murderer had deprived her of ever knowing her father and had broken Ruby Bates Winchester's heart.

That alone was reason enough to find his killer. That and all the lost possibilities.

"So how did all this get you suspended?" her mother asked after her third tequila drink.

McCall had finished her first but had passed on a second because she was driving. Even one tequila had loosened her tongue. Or maybe it was growing up with all the lies that made her want to speak the truth now.

"I found his hunting license in the mud where the bones had been buried." She felt her mother's gaze.

"So you knew it was him that first day."

"I suspected it was him."

Ruby nodded and took a drink. "What made you keep quiet?"

"I wanted to wait until I got the DNA report before I told anyone. I also knew Grant would pull me off the case once he knew for sure it was Trace. I thought I'd have more time to try to find the killer before everything hit the fan."

Ruby seemed lost in thought. "You tell your grandmother? Is that why you went out there that first time?"

"No. I just wanted to see her before she found out about the crime lab results. I'd hoped she might know something that would help me find his killer." McCall didn't add that she'd gone to the Winchester Ranch first today to give her grandmother the news. Tequila or not, she was no fool.

"You could have told me," Ruby said, sounding hurt.

"Not until it was definite."

Her mother finished her drink and stared out at the water. "You thought I killed him."

"It crossed my mind."

Ruby shot her a disappointed look, then asked, "Where exactly did you find him?"

"On a ridge south of town within sight of the Winchester Ranch. You can't go out there. It's a crime scene. I'm sure the sheriff will have a deputy posted."

She nodded. "Who would want to do that to Trace?"

"You'd know better than me." McCall saw something like a shadow cross her mother's expression. "If there is someone you suspect…"

"No," Ruby said with a shake of her head. "Will Grant be in charge of the investigation?" she asked, looking down into her drink.

"Shouldn't he be?"

It took her mother a moment. "Maybe not."

McCall felt her mother pulling away, hiding again in the past. "Mother—"

Ruby did that little shrug of the shoulders thing she did when she'd been drinking. "He and Trace didn't get along after that mess with Sandy."

McCall already suspected that. "I doubt it will matter. Truthfully? It's a cold case. Twenty-seven years is a long time. I suspect it will be impossible to find the killer."

Did her mother look relieved?

Ruby's cell phone rang. "Speaking of the devil." She snapped open the phone. "Hello?" She listened, biting her lower lip, then said, "Thanks for letting me know, Grant."

She put the phone back in her purse, unscrewed the cap on the tequila, then as if thinking better of it, screwed it back on and balled her cup up in her fist.

"Don't lose your job over this," her mother said after a moment. "Nothing can bring Trace back. It might have been better if he'd just stayed buried. I don't want you looking for his killer."

"How can you say that? Aren't you relieved that he didn't leave you? Don't you want the person who took his life brought to justice?" McCall demanded. This was the last thing she'd expected from her mother. "I thought this man was the love of your life?"

"He's gone, McCall. Hasn't he messed up our lives enough?"

McCall stared at her mother. She could see that Ruby wished her daughter had never found the hunting license in the mud at the grave site, that Trace Winchester could be buried again and so could whatever had happened on that ridge.

But unfortunately once bodies were dug up, there was no burying them again. Even if McCall wanted to, Pepper Winchester wasn't going to rest until her favorite son's murderer was swinging from a noose.

"You know who killed him," McCall said, knowing she was thinking crazy. But she kept remembering what Patty Mason had said about the mud on her mother's pickup. Mud like on the ridge where Trace had been buried.

Ruby shook her head and sighed, suddenly looking exhausted. "Of course I don't know who killed him. But if I had to guess, I'd say it was someone Trace had pushed too far."

LUKE SANK A NAIL INTO the two-by-four and reached for another one. Restless, he'd decided to work on his house until dark. But he'd been having a hell of a time concentrating on the job.

He'd tried Buzz's cell phone a half-dozen times and left several messages. He couldn't help worrying since there had been no word.

Mostly, he was mentally kicking himself for coming back here thinking he stood half a chance with McCall. It seemed they were always on opposite sides of the fence. Now this thing with Buzz…

And yet when Luke thought about holding McCall in his arms last night, he remembered those few moments when it had felt so right. His kiss had taken her by surprise, but she'd responded and he'd felt the heat in her, that old spark of desire that had flickered like a campfire between them.

He reminded himself that she'd thought he'd run her off the road. It was like dousing himself in ice water.

Just as McCall believed he'd done something unforgivable ten years ago, and even though he'd sworn he hadn't… Yeah, trust was a huge issue between them and he doubted there was anything he could do to fix that.

But he couldn't bear the thought that McCall might be in danger and worried what might be going on. Buzz wasn't stupid enough to try to run her off the road, was he?

Luke realized he didn't know anymore. He had so many questions, and his uncle was the only one who could answer them.

Restless, he started to try Buzz's cell phone again when he heard a vehicle coming up the road. Probably Buzz, he thought with relief.

Luke shaded his eyes as he watched the cloud of dust draw closer. Definitely a pickup, just not Buzz's new one he drove.

Squinting into the sun, he saw the sheriff's department logo on the side and couldn't believe his eyes.

McCall?

He watched her drive into his yard, hoping this was a social visit, knowing it probably wasn't. Had something happened to Buzz and Eugene and she was here to give him the bad news? No, the sheriff would have called, not sent McCall.

He stood in the shade as she climbed out of her pickup. Her dark hair shone in the fading sunlight. She moved with long-legged grace toward him. And as always, he was hit with such a need for this woman that it almost dropped him to his knees.

Turning back to his work, he drove a nail into another two-by-four, warning himself not to get his hopes up that her being here had anything to do with him. Or that kiss last night.

Chapter Ten

McCall followed the sound of the hammer toward the wooden structure etched against the sunset—and Luke Crawford.

She'd driven her mother back to town in time to get ready for Ruby's date with Red Harper.

"Are you sure you're up to going out tonight?" she'd asked her mother, trying to hide her surprise. "I could rent a movie, get us a pizza—"

"No." Ruby had patted McCall's arm. "I need to see Red. I want to be the one to tell him."

McCall still didn't know how her mother was really taking the news of her husband's murder. Maybe it hadn't sunk in yet. Or maybe it had and she'd been serious about McCall dropping her investigation. "Sure. Whatever you want."

"Your father's been dead to me for a long time," Ruby had said. "I guess I just need time, you know?"

McCall had guessed so. Everyone in town would be talking about Trace's murder. Being the woman left alone and pregnant didn't garner the same kind of sympathy as being the widow of a man unjustly murdered in his prime. Ruby hadn't gotten to be the grieving widow. Until now.

Normally, McCall would have headed to her cabin, anxious for the peace and quiet. But it was still early and there'd been one more thing she had to do.

The sun had slipped behind the Little Rockies as she spotted Luke. She glanced past him and the skeletal frame of his house to the stock pond in the distance and felt a chill snake up her spine.

Her gaze came back to Luke, and for a moment, she wanted to stop all this. She wanted to sit down in the shade with Luke, share a cold beer, watch the sun set and forget about the past, all of it, especially the part where Luke broke her heart.

She realized she shouldn't have come here feeling so vulnerable. For years, she'd built a shield around herself after Luke hurt her. But there were now cracks in her armor. Finding out that her father hadn't run out on her and her mother had opened old wounds—just as Luke had by coming back to Whitehorse.

Luke's presence had filled her head with thoughts of what could have been. What could still be if only she could forgive him.

She listened to Luke pound another nail and shelved all her crazy thoughts, especially the ones about Luke Crawford and second chances.

The air was cool in the shade. The hammering stopped. She knew Luke had already seen her coming.

As he slipped his hammer into the side of his carpenter's apron, he turned and leaned against the opening where he'd been working. "McCall," he said, the sound of it making her ache.

He looked wary, but who could blame him after last night? She bristled, reminded that all she'd done to him was slap him. Nothing compared to a kiss. She was the one who should be wary.

The sun lit in his dark eyes. His skin looked bronze against his pale yellow shirt, the sleeves rolled up to expose strong forearms. The jeans were worn, just like the boots.

He couldn't have looked more appealing or more dangerous to her equilibrium, she thought as she gazed up at him.

"What brings you out here, Deputy?" he asked.

That earlier thought of sitting in the shade with him flitted past. She swatted it away. "Your stock pond."

Luke smiled as if he thought she was kidding. He dropped the nails he'd been holding into a pocket of the carpenter's apron. "You looking to do some fishing? There's northern pike in there as long as your arm. But shouldn't you have brought your fishing pole?"

"That's not what I'm fishing for."

He raised a brow and pushed back his straw Western hat to reveal a thick pencil stuck behind his right ear. He smelled of sawdust.

"How deep would you say the pond is?" she asked, trying to distract herself from how good Luke looked and the way being this close to him made her ache.

His lips quirked in a questioning grin, humor sparkling in his dark eyes. "At the dam end? Twelve to fourteen feet. Shallower at the other end."

She nodded. Plenty deep enough. She felt a shiver of dread ripple through her. Her father's pickup was in that stock pond. With the Crawford Ranch vacant twenty-seven years ago it was the perfect place to dispose of the truck quickly.

Nor was there any reason it would have been found since the place had been bought by an out-of-state corporation and had quickly gotten tied up in some legal mess before Luke bought it back.

"Then you don't mind if I have a look?" she asked.

"Sure. What is it you're looking for anyway?"

"I've got this crazy idea there might be a pickup down there."

"In the pond?" He sounded skeptical as he untied his carpenter's apron and dropped it on the floor before he jumped down and walked with her toward the earthen dam.

As they approached, she saw that the water was the color of a rusted pickup, much too dark to see anything in its depths.

"How are you planning to— Whoa," he said as she took off her jacket and pulled off one boot. "You aren't aiming to jump in there?"

"You know of a better way to find out if the truck is down there?"

"That water will be ice-cold. It's spring fed."

She pulled off her other boot and began to unbuckle the belt on her jeans.

"*Stop.* As curious as I am to see how far you're willing to go with this, I can't let you," Luke said.

"I can get a warrant—"

"I'm not talking about *that.*" He was angry with her again. "Damn it, McCall, if there's something in there, I'll find out. Whose pickup is this you think is down there, anyway?"

"My father's."

Luke blinked. "Trace Winchester?"

"He *is* my father, no matter what the local grapevine says."

"I didn't mean— Never mind." He pulled off his boots, tossing them down, then unsnapped his shirt and dropped it into the pile. She tried not to look at his bare chest.

Nor had she meant to make him angry with her again. "I can do this without your help," she said, although she hadn't been looking forward to going in that water.

He leveled his gaze on her, eyes hard as stones. "I don't doubt you're more than capable and determined to do anything you set your mind to and that you certainly don't need me, but it's *my* stock pond. Stay here." In his socks, he padded around the dam to the side and waded gingerly into the water.

She could tell that the water was freezing cold from the way he tried not to show just how uncomfortable it was. When he reached chest-deep, he did a shallow dive and disappeared beneath the still dark surface.

McCall took off her good leather belt and dropped it on the ground, ready to go in after him if necessary. A meadowlark sang from the sage. In the distance, a truck shifted down on Highway 191. Nothing moved on the stock pond's surface.

McCall held her breath as she stared down at the water and waited.

No Luke.

She would give him just a little longer and then—

He surfaced in a shower of dirty water and swam hard toward the side, his back to her. As he climbed out, his jeans running water, she saw something in the set of his shoulders. And felt herself sag under the knowledge.

"It's down there, isn't it?" she asked as he climbed up to the dam and picked up his shirt.

LUKE SHRUGGED INTO HIS SHIRT, the thin fabric sticking to his wet skin and fought off the chill of the water—and what he'd found.

"There's a pickup down there," he said. "And it's been there for a while. That's all I can tell you."

The radio in her patrol pickup squawked. She leaned down to pull on her boots, picked up her belt and jacket and headed toward her patrol SUV without a word.

Luke swore under his breath as she called back after a moment, "I have to go. Can I trust you not to disturb the site?"

Luke picked up his boots and walked over to her, fighting his temper. When was the woman going to start trusting him?

"What do you think I'm going to do? Drain the pond? Or drag the pickup out before you get back?" he asked between clenched teeth.

Her look said that's exactly what had crossed her mind.

He shook his head, his anger suddenly spent. "McCall, why would I do that?"

"I just want to do this the legal way," she said, and he realized she wasn't wearing her badge and her gun. Why was that? "Do I need to get a warrant before I come back with a wrecker to pull out the pickup?"

"No, it's all yours."

He watched her drive away, swearing to himself. That damned woman. When he'd first seen her drive into the place he'd thought— Oh, hell, it didn't matter what he'd thought or worse, what he'd hoped. She hadn't come to see him. She was just being a cop—even if she wasn't wearing her gun or badge.

As he stomped over to the small trailer he lived in until he got his house built, he wished he'd let her go in that ice-cold pond. *Would have served her right,* he thought, his stiff jeans so cold against his skin they felt as if they were starting to freeze.

He stripped out of his clothes on his front step since he had all the privacy in the world way out here. Stark naked, he went inside and turned on the shower. As he stepped under the warm spray, he waited for it to take away some of the chill.

With McCall gone, his mind began to clear.

Trace Winchester's pickup was in his stock pond?

What had made McCall even suspect there *might* be a truck down there?

He told himself it had nothing to do with him. The place had been vacant since his parents' deaths. Luke turned off the shower and reached for a towel, finally getting why McCall had thought he might interfere with her crime scene. If that's what it was.

Buzz. McCall had been investigating him in regard to her father, and now apparently she thought the pickup in the Crawford stock pond was Trace Winchester's.

And if it was her father's truck, what the hell did that mean? Luke didn't like the implications.

Trace could have dumped the pickup before he took off for parts unknown. Or he could be inside the cab at the bottom of that pond. If so, there was little chance he'd driven himself in there by accident.

As Luke glanced out at the pond, he felt sick. A breeze riffled the surface of the water. Walleye chop, Buzz would have called it.

Buzz. Did this have something to do with his uncle? McCall apparently thought so. Luke hoped not as he reached for his cell phone and punched in Buzz's number.

Giving his uncle a heads-up wasn't interfering with the deputy or her possible crime scene. He owed Buzz at least that.

And he wanted to be the one to tell his uncle. Or maybe he wanted to judge for himself what Buzz's involvement might be based on the tone of his voice when he heard about the pickup being found in the pond.

"YOU WHAT?" SHERIFF GRANT Sheridan looked pale under the fluorescent lighting in his office.

"I believe I've found my father's pickup, the black Chevy missing since his disappearance," McCall said.

"Where the hell—"

"It was dumped in a stock pond not far from where his remains were found," she said.

Grant had been standing, but now he lowered himself into his office chair and motioned for her to sit down. "I thought I told you to stay away from this investigation?"

McCall stared at the sheriff. His color had returned but he still looked upset. Because she'd interfered with the investigation? Or because she'd found the pickup when he'd thought no one ever would? She realized that she was looking at everyone as a suspect.

"Aren't you going to ask where the stock pond is located?" she asked him.

His eyes narrowed. "I was getting to that. You realize

I can have you arrested after I told you specifically to stay clear of this investigation?"

"Are you sure you want that kind of publicity given that it's my father who was murdered and that I'm the one who found his grave *and* his pickup?"

"You're treading on thin ice, McCall. If you don't want to lose your job—"

"The stock pond is on the old Crawford place," she said, in case there was any doubt that she didn't give a damn about her job at this point. "The ranch was vacant twenty-seven years ago. Buzz Crawford had sold it, but the new out-of-state owners never took possession." Had Buzz known that might be the case?

Grant leaned back, worry creasing his forehead as he studied her. "Have you told your mother or your grandmother about the truck?"

"No. I came straight to you. I think it would be best if neither of them was notified until there is no doubt it is his pickup. Right now it's stuck in the mud about six to eight feet underwater."

"I don't want word getting out on this," the sheriff said.

"That's why I didn't go through the dispatcher. I thought we could get Tommy over at T&T Towing to pull it out. I've already gotten permission from the new owner of the property—Luke Crawford—so a warrant isn't necessary. But I would suggest we do this now before anyone else finds out. I want to be there when you bring up the pickup."

McCall knew she had overstepped her boundaries. She half expected her boss to tell her that not only didn't he give a damn about her suggestions, but he was also locking her up for obstructing his investigation.

To her surprise, he rose from his seat, picked up his coat on the way out the door, saying, "You better turn in your vehicle and ride with me. I can give you a ride home."

LUKE SAT IN THE SHADE, drinking a cold beer and watching the road into his place. He hadn't been able to reach his uncle and he was growing more concerned by the minute.

In the distance, he saw vehicles coming up the ranch road. Dust rose behind them into the twilight and floated south on the light breeze.

A perfect spring evening. Unless a pickup had been found in your stock pond that might belong to the missing father of the woman you loved—and lost.

As the tow truck roared into the yard followed by the sheriff's patrol SUV, Luke rose, put down the beer he'd hardly touched and watched the sheriff climb out. Grant Sheridan had an even grimmer expression on his face than usual.

Deputy McCall Winchester climbed out of the other side.

"I understand you've given McCall permission to drag your stock pond?" the sheriff asked.

Luke nodded. "Like I told her, it's all yours." He saw McCall glance around as if looking for someone. It hit him: she'd expected him to call Buzz to warn him. And damned if he hadn't. Would Buzz be here now if he had reached him—or on his way to South America via Mexico?

In retrospect, he was glad he hadn't reached him. The way Buzz felt about McCall and the Winchesters, he thought it better to let this play out before Buzz got the news. He didn't want Buzz making matters worse. It would be bad enough if that really was Trace Winchester's pickup buried in the mud of his stock pond—and Buzz knew something about it.

As they followed the tow truck down to the stock pond, Luke couldn't help but notice how nervous McCall was. He doubted anyone else had noticed since she hid it well.

But he knew her intimately. Even making love once changed things between a man and woman. Especially when that woman was McCall. She kept so much of herself hidden behind her tough-girl attitude. Only once had she let down her guard with him. No wonder she'd hated him after she'd thought he'd betrayed her.

"You sure you want to see this?" he asked McCall now as the sheriff went over to talk to the tow truck driver and his assistant, who was suiting up for the dive.

McCall looked over at him, frowning as if she didn't understand his concern. "My father's body isn't in the truck."

"You're sure about that?" he asked, studying her. If she was telling the truth, then why was she so nervous? Whose body did she think was going to be in there?

The diver disappeared under the water with a light, only to return moments later to come back for the cable.

Luke watched McCall out of the corner of his eye as the diver slipped under the surface. He reappeared after a short time and signaled the tow truck driver. The cable tightened as the engine mounted on the back of the tow truck began to rev.

Something moved below the surface of the water sending up bubbles then waves that lapped at the shore. Out of the rust-colored water a large pickup-shaped object emerged.

Chapter Eleven

Dark water ran from pickup, gushing to the ground as McCall tried to see what was inside the cab. But the interior was a cave of darkness behind the slimed-over windows.

She felt Grant's hand on her arm.

"Remember the deal we made," the sheriff reminded her. "You got to come along but you stay out of it."

She nodded and took a step back as he walked over to the truck and rubbed off some of the slime to check the color. McCall had already seen that it was black. A 1983 Chevy pickup. Just like the one her father had been driving the day he disappeared.

As the water draining from the cab slowed, Grant glanced back at her. With deliberate motions, he pulled on a pair of latex gloves, then reached to open the passenger's side door.

McCall gasped as a large object swept out from the pickup on a wave of dirty water.

"What the hell?" the sheriff cried, jumping back.

McCall couldn't help herself. She stepped forward as if propelled by an invisible force, stopping short when she recognized what had been at the center of the sludge.

Waterlogged, mud-filled boots had apparently been wrapped up in a wool plaid hunting coat.

She stepped past Grant to look into the cab of the pickup but couldn't tell what else might be in there, given all the sludge.

Stumbling back, she was surprised when she felt strong arms steady her.

"Easy," Luke said.

She hadn't realized she was trembling until she felt him put an arm around her and lead her away from the truck and into the shade of his house he was building.

For a moment, she stood in his embrace, then, fearful at how wonderful it felt, moved just far enough away that he wasn't touching her, cursing her stupid pride.

Luke dusted off a spot on some lumber beside the house. "Here, sit in the shade."

She sat, feeling faint and touched by his concern for her. "I hadn't expected…" Words deserted her.

"Seeing the pickup like that must have been a shock," he said quietly as he sat down beside her—just not too close.

She'd known the pickup would be her father's black Chevy. She just hadn't known it would have this effect on her. The truck looked nothing like it had in the only photo she had of her father.

So why did it hurt so much just looking at it?

Because she knew the last person to drive it hadn't been her father—but his killer.

For a moment earlier though, she'd feared that what washed out was the remains of Geneva Cavanaugh Cherry.

She could hear Grant putting in a call to the crime lab. Now the team would have even more evidence to work with in the cold-case murder investigation. But McCall doubted there would be anything to find, given how long the pickup had been under the dirty water. Even if they did find something, she wouldn't be privy to it.

"Do you want to get out of here?" Luke asked.

She nodded and rose, turning her back on the scene beside the pond. "I just need to know if his rifle is in there."

"I'll find out. Stay here."

She stood facing the Little Rockies, the sunset rimming the mountains in deepening shades of orange and pink. A shadow began to settle over the land, over her. Seeing the pickup had made it real.

McCall started at Luke's touch.

"The rifle wasn't in the pickup," he said as they headed toward his truck. "They're talking about dragging the pond."

She nodded. She hadn't expected the rifle to be in the truck. Nor did she believe they'd find it at the bottom of the pond. All along she'd suspected the killer had taken it.

"McCall!" the sheriff called after her.

She stopped and waited as he came over to where she stood. Luke continued to his truck to wait for her, leaving the two of them alone.

"Why did you ask about your father's rifle?" Grant wanted to know.

"Because he had it with him that day. He'd gone hunting."

"You're sure he had the rifle? I thought he'd been ticketed the day before for poaching?"

"He had, but for some reason Buzz Crawford hadn't confiscated the rifle—or his antelope tag." She saw the sheriff's surprised expression. "Buzz says he doesn't recall, too long ago. But I checked. Buzz never turned the rifle in to the Fish and Game evidence department, and my mother swears Trace had it the day he disappeared."

Grant was studying her. "How did you know the pickup was here?"

"I told you, I saw the pond from the ridge. What better place to hide the truck than a vacant ranch close by?"

The sheriff pulled off his hat and raked a hand through his graying hair. He dropped his voice as he said, "I know you talked to Sandy." His gaze searched her face. "Where were you going with this?"

"I talked to anyone who had reason to hate my father enough to kill and bury him on that ridge twenty-seven years ago."

"And you thought Sandy…" He shook his head.

"Actually, I thought you had more motive," McCall said.

All the breath seemed to whoosh out of him. *"Me?"*

"You must have hated him. Probably still do."

Grant looked away. "You're wrong. I'm thankful Trace was such an incredible bastard." His gaze came back to her. "He gave me a chance with Sandy, one I wouldn't have had otherwise."

McCall felt a deep sorrow for Grant. The man really seemed to believe that he'd won Sandy.

"This ends here for you," Grant said. "Got it?"

She didn't answer, just turned and walked toward Luke's pickup. Without a word, she slid in. As Luke pulled away, she glanced back at the pond. Her father's pickup looked like some monster dragged up from the black lagoon.

"EVERYTHING ALL RIGHT?" Luke said as he drove them away. He hadn't been able to hear the conversation between her and the sheriff, but he'd watched in the rearview mirror, and from their body language it hadn't been a pleasant discussion.

"Just great." McCall leaned back and closed her eyes. "Thanks for getting me out of there. I'm sorry about the way I acted earlier."

"You don't have to do that."

"What?"

"Pretend. I can tell this is tearing you up."

She said nothing as he turned onto Highway 191 and headed north toward Whitehorse. Luke wished she would let him help her through this, but he could tell by her silence that she'd already shut him out.

He started to turn on the radio, when her words stopped him.

"There's a reason I knew my father's body wasn't in the pickup." Her voice sounded small and filled with emotion, and when he glanced over at her he saw the tears beaded on her closed lashes. "Rocky Harrison found my father's remains not far from the stock pond."

Luke had heard about the bones from Buzz, but he'd never imagined they would turn out to be McCall's father's. Worry burrowed deeper under his skin as he recalled Buzz's interest in the find. Natural curiosity, like driving by a wreck and being forced to look? Or something more sinister?

And now Trace Winchester's pickup had been found on the old Crawford place.

Luke drove, mind racing. He wasn't sure what scared

him the most. That McCall suspected Buzz. Or that she actually might have reason to.

"You're not wearing your badge or your gun," he said after a moment.

She opened her eyes and sat up, turning away to wipe her tears. "I'm suspended for two weeks. I withheld some evidence until I was certain the remains were my father's."

Luke couldn't imagine what she'd been going through. "I'm sorry." He knew the words weren't near enough. Throwing caution to the wind, he reached over and took her hand. He expected her to pull away and was surprised when her hand closed tightly onto his.

She made an undecipherable sound. He could feel her pain. But it was the anger and frustration he felt coming off her in waves that worried him. He knew this woman.

"I know what you're planning to do," he said as the road topped a hill and he could see the dark outline of the trees that meandered through the Milk River Valley. A few lights from town glittered faintly in the growing darkness.

McCall turned to give him an amused smile. He could tell she didn't think he knew anything about her. She couldn't have been more wrong.

"I know you're going after your father's killer."

"You witnessed my discussion with the sheriff. If I get involved I'll be fired."

Luke chuckled. "Like that will stop you." He saw the determination in her expression. "It won't bring your father back."

"No, there's no changing the past, is there?"

He glanced over at her, wondering if she was talking about the two of them or her father's murder.

"I have to find his killer. It's the only justice he's

going to get." He could feel her gaze on him. "Why? Worried where my investigation is going to lead me?"

"Buzz didn't kill your father," he said, hoping the hell he was right.

"And you know that how?"

"What was his motive?"

"He had it in for my father."

Luke thought about all the tickets Buzz had written Trace. It certainly looked that way. But murder? "Do you have any proof?"

"Not yet."

"What if you're wrong about Buzz?" *Just as you're wrong about me,* he thought as he drove through town and took the river road to her cabin.

"One way or another, I intend to get justice for my father," she said.

He didn't like the sound of that. He pulled up next to her cabin.

"Thanks for the ride," McCall said and started to open her door. "If you're so sure your uncle is innocent, then get me a copy of Buzz's daily log for those two days. The day before hunting season opened and opening day."

Luke swore. "I can't do that."

"I know you can. But I understand why you wouldn't want to. Don't worry, I'll find another way," she said, climbing out and slamming his pickup door.

"Wait," he called as he reached over, opened his glove box and took out the Colt .45. Opening his door, he went after her. He knew this woman, knew she would move heaven and earth to find her father's killer. Nothing could stop her. Especially him.

But he couldn't let her do it alone—or unarmed—no matter where the trail led.

"I'll help you." His words surprised him as much as her. If she tried to get copies of that logbook, the sheriff would find out and she would be fired—if not arrested. He couldn't let that happen.

He grabbed her arm and turned her around to face him. Touching her was like sending a bolt of electricity through him. He felt the surge of desire rush through his veins and prepared himself for the powerful ache it left when she pulled free.

She didn't pull free this time. Her eyes locked with his. *"Why?"*

He knew she was asking more than why he would help her.

"You know why," he said as he let go of her arm. "You're the reason I came back here. The only reason."

A BANK OF LOW CLOUDS MADE the night darker than normal as McCall watched Luke turn and leave. She felt shaken to her core. He'd come back here because of her?

The tall black limbs of the cottonwood trees creaked and groaned in the breeze against a sky as dark as the inside of a body bag.

She hugged herself against the cool breeze and breathed in the scents of the night, trying to clear her head. His confession changed nothing, she told herself, and yet she knew it did.

Suddenly she felt as if she was being propelled headlong into disaster, no longer in control of anything and completely unable to stop what was about to happen.

"Damn you, Luke," she whispered as the pickup's taillights disappeared into the darkness.

McCall rubbed a hand over her face. She was exhausted from lack of sleep, her body ached from her crash into the ditch the night before and she was frustrated and confused.

Luke was so sure his uncle was innocent.

Was she that sure that Buzz had killed her father? All she had was circumstantial evidence at best. Anyone would have known about the old Crawford place being vacant. Anyone could have taken Trace's rifle after killing him.

Nothing she'd learned had moved her any closer to finding her father's killer. She'd learned things about her mother she hadn't wanted to know and even worse things about her father.

Her job had been jeopardized, and she wasn't even sure she wanted it back now. Maybe worst of all, she had the feeling there was no one she could trust. She'd burned bridges with everyone she knew, and now Luke had her questioning where this obsession had taken her.

She couldn't change the past. Her father was dead. Even her mother was trying to move on.

All McCall had done was stir up a hornet's nest that had left her alienated from people she cared about.

She felt like crying and had to fight the tears, knowing that once she started she might not be able to stop.

It wasn't the cold temperature tonight that chilled her to the bone as she listened to Luke drive away. She needed him, wanted him, thought she couldn't stand another night without him.

She turned, aching to call him back, wanting desperately to quit pushing him away. Their lovemaking came back to her in a rush, the feel of his body against hers, the gentle sweet way he'd made love to her.

It had been magic, bonding them together in a way she realized that had never been broken. Neither of them had been able to move on.

The past reared its ugly head, but no longer had the power it had held over her. Luke had sworn that he hadn't gone to high school the next day and bragged about "nailing" her. She'd been so hurt, so confused, so heartbroken. It had seemed so unlike him to brag to his friends but there had only been the two of them down by the river that night. It had been their secret. Word had spread the way it always had in Whitehorse, and her reputation had been ruined, though that was the least of it.

McCall had lost faith in men and love and Luke Crawford in particular. He'd betrayed her and that betrayal had kept her from trusting another man again.

Her cell phone rang, making her jump. She checked it and saw that it was a pay phone. "Hello?"

"You want to know who killed your old man?" said a low hoarse voice, clearly disguised. "Why don't you ask your mother?"

"Who is this?" She realized she'd stopped walking toward her cabin.

"Ask her about the black eye she was sporting the last time anyone saw Trace Winchester and who gave it to her."

McCall flinched as if she'd been hit. "Are you saying my father hit her?"

A chuckle. "Only because she got in the way. He was trying to hit her *boyfriend*." The line went dead.

McCall swore under her breath. *Black eye? Boy-*

friend? She realized she was still carrying the gun Luke had pressed into her hand. Turning, she headed for her SUV.

With luck she could catch her mother before she went out on her date with Red Harper.

"IS SOMETHING WRONG?" Ruby repeated as McCall entered the trailer.

Everything was wrong and had been McCall's whole life. She'd felt as if everyone around her had lied to her. Now she knew it was true.

"Why don't you tell me about the black eye my father gave you," she said as she stepped into the trailer.

Ruby froze. "What?"

"My father hit you."

"No. It wasn't—" She folded the dish towel she'd been using to dry the few items on her drain board and placed it carefully on the counter. "Where would you get—"

"Or was he trying to hit your *boyfriend?*" The one thing McCall had believed all these years was that Trace Winchester had been her mother's true love. Now even that was in question.

Ruby chewed at her lower lip before reaching for her cigarettes. McCall beat her to them, tossing the pack aside.

"How about the truth for once?"

Her mother shook her head. "There were things I didn't want to tell you. I wanted to spare you."

Ruby turned to open the fridge. "You want a Diet Coke?" She must have seen McCall's impatient expression, because she pulled only one out, popped the top and took a drink.

"Trace and I were having problems," Ruby said

finally. "I told you about his mother cutting off his money, trying to rein him back in. He was torn. She wouldn't relent. We were broke. I was pregnant and sick and not working as much...." She took another drink, her throat working.

McCall recalled what Patty had told her about the morning her mother showed up at the café late. She'd thought from the mud on the old pickup that Ruby had been out looking for Trace.

"You said the last time you saw him was the morning of opening day when he went antelope hunting," McCall reminded her and saw her mother's face flush under the weight of the lie.

Patty had said her mother came in late and it was plain as her face that she and Trace had had a fight. McCall had thought Patty meant: plain as the look on her face, but she must have been talking about Ruby's black eye.

Her mother started to cry. "Trace used to put his hand on my stomach and just light up when he felt you move. It was his idea to name you McCall after his father, even if you were a girl." She smiled through her tears. "He would have settled down once you were born. Would have been fine if—"

"The black eye, Mother."

Ruby finished the soda, tossed the can in the recycle bin McCall had forced on her and motioned to one of the kitchen chairs. McCall had been leaning against the kitchen counter, blocking her mother's path.

She moved now, allowing Ruby to sit down, but she could tell her mother was itching for a cigarette.

"I was fine when Trace was home, but when he wasn't..." Ruby said, turning the ashtray in a circle with her finger. "I did something terrible." Her voice cracked like the ice on Nelson Reservoir in the spring. "I went out on Trace."

"Went *out?*"

"It was just that one time. I swear. We regretted it right away."

"*We?*"

Her mother kept turning the ashtray, refusing to look at her.

"When did this happen?"

"The night before opening day."

McCall swore. "So you didn't see him the next morning, did you? You don't even know if he had his rifle or not." She couldn't believe this. She'd based all her assumptions about his killer on who had taken the rifle from Trace and when.

Ruby stopped spinning the ashtray. "Trace came home the night before opening day, caught us and took a punch at him. I got in the middle."

McCall sighed. Would the saga of her parents never end? "No wonder you thought he'd left you. Who is the other man, Mother?"

Ruby looked away and McCall knew. A cold chill worked its way up her spine. "It was Red, wasn't it?"

Her mother burst into tears.

Now it all made sense. Why Red hadn't asked Ruby out all these years. It had been guilt. He and Ruby had both blamed themselves for Trace leaving.

"Even if he hadn't gotten himself killed, he would have left me," Ruby cried. "Now you know why. It was *my* fault."

McCall stepped to her mother, squatting down to

hug her. Ruby shook with shuddering sobs, her tears hot against McCall's cheek.

"He married you. He wouldn't have if he hadn't loved you," McCall whispered. It didn't matter if it was true or not. Not anymore. The truth was that Trace had never left Ruby. Never left either of them.

The sobs slowed. Ruby sniffed, wiped her tears.

McCall sat down across from her, feeling closer to her mother than she had in years. Ruby had cheated. It wasn't the first time a woman had done such a thing nor would it be the last. There were worse sins. Like murder.

McCall didn't stop her mother this time when she reached for her cigarettes.

"I'm sorry. I'm so sorry," Ruby said after taking a long drag and blowing the smoke out the side of her mouth, waving her hand as if that would save her daughter from the secondhand smoke.

It was hard to tell exactly what her mother was sorry for. Tricking Trace. Getting pregnant. Marrying Trace. Cheating on him. Or believing for years that her infidelity was the reason he was gone.

Whatever Ruby was sorry for, she'd paid for it the past twenty-seven years.

McCall drove home, wanting nothing more than to sleep for twenty-four hours. The cold night air did nothing to chase away her fatigue. The river bottom was quiet, the low clouds of the spring sky overhead a deep ebony.

Rounding the corner of the deck, she was almost to the door when something moved in the darkness. McCall froze as a dark shape came across the deck at her.

Chapter Twelve

As Eugene Crawford stepped from the shadows, McCall knew he'd been waiting for her.

Her stomach tightened as she reached for her weapon only to realize she wasn't wearing it and she'd left the gun Luke had given her in the truck.

As she reached in her pocket for her cell phone, Eugene stepped in front of her, blocking her path with one big, heavy arm and slapping her cell out of her hand. It skittered across the deck and disappeared over the side.

"You bitch." Anger contorted his ruddy, thick features. "Because of you my uncle was arrested for murder."

The sheriff had arrested Buzz for her father's murder? Grant was so cautious he wouldn't have done that without sufficient evidence. He must have found something in Trace's pickup.

"I know you framed my old man," Eugene said, shoving her back against the wall of the house.

She could smell alcohol on his breath and warned herself to be careful of this dangerous man. Eugene outweighed her by a hundred pounds and had a mean streak that she'd seen all through grade school. In high school he'd asked her out, and when she'd turned him down, he'd done everything he could to make her life miserable behind Luke's back.

McCall had known that arresting him the other night at the bar would come back to haunt her. Here he was spoiling for a fight again, only he planned to win this one.

She tried to remain calm, not easy when they both knew that they were all alone out here. Even if she screamed no one would hear her, and Eugene was too big to fight.

"I'm sorry, Eugene, but I don't know what you're talking about," she said, trying to keep her voice calm.

"*Right*. You wouldn't know anything about him getting arrested and hauled off to jail for murdering the man your mother claimed fathered you."

McCall held her ground although it was hard with Eugene Crawford this close and reeking of alcohol, sweat and anger, but she knew that any show of fear would feed his need to hurt someone. And tonight that someone was her.

"If the sheriff arrested Buzz, then he must have his reasons," she said, and started to move past him.

He stopped her, slapping one large beefy palm onto the wall next to her, trapping her. He leaned in. "You always did have a mouth on you."

McCall feared how this was going to end. "You might want to consider that you are threatening an officer of the law, Eugene. Do you really need that kind of trouble?"

"After the trouble I'm already in?" He laughed, a harsh, spittle-filled laugh. "You ain't no deputy. That's right, word's out about you." He let his gaze slide down her body. "That's why you aren't wearing your gun."

"I'm only suspended. Technically—"

"Let me tell you what you can do with your *technicalities*," Eugene grabbed a handful of her hair in his fist, making her eyes water with the pain. "I got news for you—you were always a tramp just like your mother."

"Easy, those are fighting words," she said on a painful breath and clenched her right hand into a fist as she remembered the satisfaction she'd felt when she'd slugged this bully back in grade school for words along that same line.

Eugene sneered at her, egging her on. He wanted her to hit him so he could take some of his meanness out on her.

"This must have been a red-letter week for you," he said. "Locked up *two* Crawfords. Bet you'd like to see Luke behind bars, too, wouldn't you."

"Eugene, I have nothing against any of the Crawfords."

"You mean against *Luke*. Oh, that's right. He used to be the man of your dreams. But I took care of that. You remember in high school?" Eugene asked. "That night down by the river?"

She felt her stomach drop. The night she and Luke had made love.

"You thought he was the one who went to school the next day and bragged about bagging you," Eugene said, grinning viciously.

Luke hadn't lied. It had been Eugene. Luke had sworn he hadn't said anything. But how could she have believed him? How could she when no one else had known about the two of them making love by the campfire.

At least that's what she'd thought.

"You destroyed my reputation in high school just to

get back at me for not going out with you?" Her voice broke, trembling with rage. Eugene had destroyed more than her reputation. He'd destroyed what she and Luke had shared and every dream they had of being together, not to mention her broken heart.

McCall would have tried to take Eugene on, throwing everything she had at him, even though she knew she couldn't win and would come out of the fight the worse for wear.

The only thing that stopped her was the dark figure that appeared at the edge of the deck.

"I followed the two of you," Eugene was saying, "Saw you beside the campfire." He let out a low whistle. "I said right then that I would have some of that one day," he said, gripping her hair tighter, unaware that they were no longer alone. "Guess that day has arrived." His free hand grabbed the neck of her shirt and ripped it downward.

"Get your hands off her!"

Eugene whirled at the sound of Luke's voice behind him. The look of fear on his face was almost enough retribution. Almost.

"*You* were the one who started the rumor about McCall," Luke said between clenched teeth, confirming that he'd heard. There was a cold fury in his voice.

Eugene must have heard it, too, because he released her and stepped back, raising both hands in surrender.

Why had Luke come back? Not that it mattered. She'd never been so glad to see him.

"Cousin," Eugene said, sounding alarmed. "It isn't what you think."

"I *think* you were about to rape McCall, but I asked you

a question. Did you just say you were the one who started the rumor about me and McCall?" Luke demanded.

Trapped, Eugene went on the defensive, turning belligerent and confrontational. "You should be thanking me. I did you the biggest favor of your life and you didn't even know it. You could have ended up with this slut if it hadn't been for me."

LUKE FELT AS IF HE'D BEEN sucker punched when he'd heard Eugene confess to what he'd done. "Do you have any idea what you did?" He took a step toward his cousin.

"Come on," Eugene said, taking a step back. "If she slept with you, she slept with everyone else in high school. She wanted what I was going to give her tonight. She asked for it."

Luke punched him, knocking Eugene down, and advanced ready to kick the hell out of him. He wanted to tear Eugene limb from limb. He'd never felt this kind of rage.

"What the—?" Eugene said, scrambling to his feet. "I was like a brother to you. She's a *Winchester*. A friggin' Winchester. I—"

Luke reached for Eugene, right hand balled into a fist and ready to strike again.

McCall grabbed his arm. "You don't want to do this," she said quietly.

"You're wrong about that," Luke said, breathing hard. "You heard him. His jealousy destroyed what we could have had. All these years…"

He started to pull free of her, half-afraid that once he started in on Eugene he might not be able to stop, and knowing it wouldn't change what had torn him and McCall apart.

"Eugene just started the rumors, Luke. I didn't trust you enough to know you were telling me the truth. And once the lies started…"

Eugene was cowering at the edge of the deck.

Luke fought to control his temper and stepped back. "Get out of my sight, Eugene, or I swear…"

His cousin scrambled over the railing, dropping the few feet to the ground and was gone into the night.

It took a moment for Luke to calm down. When he turned to McCall, he saw there were tears in her eyes.

"I should have believed you," she said.

He shook his head. "We thought we were alone. We were young, and what we had together that night scared us both." He drew her into the shelter of his arms and she snuggled against him. "I couldn't bear it though that you thought I would betray you. After that…" He was unable to put into words how miserable he'd been, how miserable he still was without her. "You should have let me kick his ass. If I hadn't come back to your cabin when I did…"

"Luke, I'm okay." She stepped back from his embrace as if she needed to get her equilibrium, to reassure herself that she was fine, that she could take care of herself.

Eugene had scared her, made her feel defenseless, and Luke knew that was a feeling McCall couldn't bear.

But it wasn't Eugene, he realized, who had her running scared. It was him. He'd hoped that the truth would change everything but now feared it hadn't.

"Don't push me away," he said, but didn't touch her.

She shook her head, tears welling in her eyes. "It was high school," she said, confirming what he'd guessed had her so afraid.

Had what they'd felt for each other back then been real? Or had they built it up in their minds, making more of it than it was? Was she that afraid to find out if those feelings for each other were still there?

"I came back here tonight because I can't bear to let any more time go by," Luke said. "For hell's sake, stop pushing me away, McCall."

MCCALL KNEW THAT IF SHE let him walk away this time, it would be the last chance for them. "I don't want you to go."

He stared at her as if afraid to trust her words. Both of them were still afraid of being hurt again; she could see it in his eyes.

But neither could deny the electricity that arced between them, she thought. The air seemed to vibrate around them. She could almost hear the low hum in the cold night air. She didn't dare touch him. Didn't dare move.

She could see in his face the same battle that was going on inside him. Had that night they'd made love so long ago just been puppy love? Nothing more?

They would never know if she let him walk away now.

"Please," she whispered and closed her eyes as he reached out and cupped the back of her neck with his large warm hand. A quiver shuddered through her as he tightened his fingers on her nape and slowly drew her to him.

Her heart seemed to stop, then take off. Heat rushed through her. Her breath came in a rush as he dragged her against his firm, solid body. She could feel the pounding of his heart.

He held her like that, his breath ragged. She heard him swallow and finally opened her eyes to look up at him.

"McCall," he whispered as he swept her up into his arms and into the cabin, kicking the door closed behind them.

As he lowered her to her feet, she slid down his body until he found her mouth. She caught her breath as he kissed her with a passion that had her toes curling in her boots.

His fingers entwined in her long hair, and her pulse thundered under her skin as he deepened the kiss. She felt his hand on her cheek, then her throat. As he released her mouth, she threw back her head and felt his fingers, then his mouth leave a hot trail down her throat to the torn opening of her shirt.

She gasped as she felt his hand cup her breast, the rough pad of his thumb rubbing her already pebble-hard nipple until she cried out, heat rushing to her center. He freed her breasts and covered them in turn with his mouth, dropping to his knees.

Later she would remember unsnapping his Western shirt, running her palms over the hard muscles of his chest, working at the buttons on his jeans.

She couldn't remember shedding her clothing, only the feel of her naked flesh pressed against his as he carried her to the bedroom, saying something about this time doing it right—in a real bed.

What she would never forget was the aching heat of desire, the need that consumed her every ragged breath. She cried out when his touch released her, and the longing started building again until she thought she couldn't bear it.

She remembered the welcome weight of him, the feeling of him filling her completely and that roller-coaster ride of desire and heart-pounding pleasure before the quaking release and that experience of ultimate fulfillment.

As she lay spent beside him, his arm around her, she memorized the feel, the smell, the sound of him, wanting to keep all of it forever. Not admitting that inkling of fear that, like ten years ago, something would drive them apart—only this time forever.

A LIGHT RAIN FELL FROM the low clouds. Mist snaked up the river, wrapping the bare branches of the cotton-woods in gray gauze.

McCall stretched as she looked out on the tranquil scene. Strange how different it looked this morning. She realized that it wasn't the familiar landscape that had changed, though; it was her.

She felt new, like the spring leaves gracing the trees from her window—the only bright color along the river bottom.

Lying on her side, she sensed rather than heard Luke approach. The air pressure around her seemed to change. She waited for his touch, aching with anticipation.

His fingertips were warm across the cool flesh of her, hip as he trailed them down the slope of her waist and up along her rib cage. She sucked in a breath as his finger brushed her breast. She took in the freshly showered scent of him. His hair would still be wet and dark against the warm brown of his skin.

As he lay down on the bed, he encircled her with his arms and drew her back against him.

She smiled, a soft chuckle escaping her throat as she realized he was wonderfully naked.

"I missed you," he whispered at her ear, his breath tickling her ear.

"Hmm," she said, leaning back against him.

"You are so beautiful, McCall."

She closed her eyes. In Luke's arms, she *felt* beautiful. Felt as if this was where she had always been meant to be. She'd never understood her mother's elusive quest for true love until this moment.

Lying in her lover's arms, McCall understood what it meant to love with such passion that you felt you would die without this man. That you would do *anything* to be with him.

Luke Crawford had ignited that kind of passion in her. For years he had stayed like a brand on her skin. She knew that no matter how this ended, she would always ache for only him. No other man would ever be able to satisfy this need.

They had talked and made love late into the night, skirting around the issue of their families and the past, except for confessions that they'd never gotten over each other.

Neither talked of the future, both of them no doubt fearful that this was too fragile. McCall was afraid of spoiling this moment if it was all they had. They had both let lies keep them apart all these years. Lies and fear that they were too young to know real love. Too young to be as serious as they'd been.

Would they have made it together had Eugene not started the rumor? They would never know.

McCall had told him why she hadn't dated, how she'd been afraid after him that she would be like her mother, going from one man to another, looking for that feeling that only Luke could give her.

"I never want to let you out of my arms," he whispered next to her ear now. "It broke my heart that you thought I could hurt you that way."

She nodded, surprised at her tears.

"Oh, McCall," Luke said, turning her around to face him. He touched his thumb pad to her cheek to wipe away an errant tear before dropping his mouth to hers. She lost herself in him just as she knew she always would.

Luke's cell phone rang and he pulled back to check his phone. "It's Buzz. I'm going to have to take this," he said as he slid out of bed, pulled on his jeans and left the room.

McCall lay in the bed staring up at the log ceiling. She'd heard Luke's quick exclamation of breath before he'd left the room. Something told her he hadn't overheard that Buzz had been arrested when he saved her from Eugene last night.

When he came back into the room, she saw the change in him.

"Buzz has been arrested," he said, retrieving the rest of his clothing from where it had been dropped last night in a frenzy of passion. He looked up. "You already knew?"

"Eugene told me. That's why he was so angry. I thought you overheard. I'm sorry."

"I guess I came in late for that news," Luke said, staring at her for a long moment. His anger had ebbed, but she could feel him pulling away. Buzz was family.

McCall watched him finish dressing, already missing him and fearing he wouldn't be back. They'd always loved each other, but ten years ago it hadn't been enough. Was it now?

"You had to have seen this coming," she said, a plea in her voice. "The pickup was in the Crawford stock pond. Buzz had access and he knew no one would be around that place. Grant wouldn't have arrested Buzz without sufficient evidence."

"Your father's rifle was found in Buzz's lake house," Luke said. "What fool would keep the weapon on his premises?"

An arrogant fool. A man who thought he was above the law. A man like Buzz Crawford. Or from what she'd learned about him, a man like Trace Winchester. Is that why Buzz had hated her father so much? Because he reminded him of himself?

"You can't even be sure your father had that rifle with him when he died," Luke said. "You told me that Buzz couldn't remember if he'd taken it."

Her mother had lied about seeing Trace the opening morning of antelope season. Had she lied about seeing the rifle the last time she saw Trace?

Buzz had caught Trace poaching the day before. Maybe he had taken the rifle after all—and just not turned it in to evidence. Maybe her father had already been in the ground by the opening of antelope season.

"It all comes down to my father's rifle," she said quickly. "If Buzz confiscated it, then he probably wrote it down in his logbook the day before the opening of antelope season."

"Do you really believe that if he'd killed your father

and kept the rifle, he would have written it down?" Luke demanded.

"Buzz is arrogant enough he might have. But at least you will know if he was in the area of the ridge that day."

"Anyone could have put that rifle in Buzz's lake house. Everyone knew he never locked his front door."

Another example of Buzz's arrogance. He was daring someone to steal from him.

"Not *anyone* could have put the rifle in his house," she argued. "Only the person who took it from my father. Come on, Luke," she said, needing him on her side. "You're afraid your uncle is guilty and worried what he'll do now that it's all coming out."

His gaze softened. "I'm just trying to make sense out of all this." He stepped over to the bed. She felt her heart break at the thought that even now their families could come between them.

Sitting on the edge of the bed, he drew her to him, holding her tight. "I'm sorry. I have to go. I'll call you later?" He brushed a kiss over her lips, then his gaze met hers and held it and she saw the longing, the regret, the same fears she was feeling, before he turned and left.

Chapter Thirteen

Luke was allowed to go back to Buzz's cell rather than speak to him via the phones through the thick plastic partition.

He knew that it was because he was a game warden with the same training as any other law enforcement officer, but also because a lot of people still looked up to Buzz and his legacy.

Whitehorse was a small town where some loyalties never died. Just as grudges and slights never did.

"It's about damned time," Buzz said through the bars as Luke walked down the short hall to his cell. "I've been here all night. The sheriff was waiting for me the moment Eugene and I got back from Billings. I've been trying to call you for hours."

Luke had turned off his phone when he was with McCall and had forgotten to turn it back on until this morning. "You could have called Eugene."

"Don't get smart with me," his uncle snapped.

Right, this was about bailing him out, and Eugene wouldn't be able to raise the money.

"Why would the sheriff arrest you?" he asked, remembering what McCall had said about sufficient evidence.

"That bastard sheriff thinks I killed Trace Winchester."

"Why would he think that?"

Buzz slashed a hand through the air in frustration. "McCall Winchester framed me. Why the hell do you think?"

Luke stared at his uncle, remembering back in high school when Buzz had found out that Luke was dating McCall Winchester. Eugene, no doubt, had told him. Eugene had probably been spying on him the whole time.

Buzz had gone ballistic. "I won't have you dating Ruby Winchester's daughter." It still made no sense, this hatred of the Winchester's over some land decades ago. Even back then, Luke had felt as if this animosity was more personal.

"How could *she* frame you?" Luke asked with a sigh.

"It was her father's rifle. One day she asks me what happened to the rifle, as if I can remember that long ago, and the next the sheriff shows up at my door with a search warrant and, big surprise, finds Trace Winchester's rifle hidden in my house. Doesn't take a rocket scientist to figure it out."

The only way Buzz could have had the rifle was if he took it from Trace Winchester. Either confiscated it when he wrote him up for poaching. Or took it when he killed him on that ridge.

Buzz was a lot of things, but Luke refused to believe his uncle was a killer.

"How would McCall have gotten the rifle?" Luke asked.

"From her mother—the person who killed Trace

Winchester," Buzz said with such venom that Luke was taken aback. "She's behind all this, just getting her daughter to do her dirty work."

Luke could see that his uncle needed him to believe this. There was only one thing Luke was certain of: McCall hadn't put the rifle in Buzz's house.

"I know that look," Buzz said with a curse. "That woman's turned your head around. You've always had a weakness for the little chippie."

"Don't call her that."

"I just told you that she and her mother framed me and you're defending her?"

"And I'm telling you I don't believe it. If you locked your house—"

His uncle swore. "Just get me out of here."

"When's the bail hearing?" he asked, knowing what it would take to get his uncle out on a murder charge. Luke would have to put up his property, that's if the judge allowed bail at all.

"The hearing's this morning. Make sure I don't spend another night in jail, you hear? You owe me that."

Luke looked at the man who'd raised him, reminded himself of the sacrifices Buzz had made over the years and bit back a reply he knew he would regret.

"Just a minute," Buzz said as Luke started to leave. "The other day on the phone on my way to Billings… Why were you asking about my old pickup?"

"Someone's been using it for poaching deer along the Milk."

Buzz swore, but it didn't have his usual intensity. Nor did he seem as shocked and angry by the news as Luke had thought he would be.

He felt dread settle deeper in his gut. "Is there anything you want to tell me before I see about getting you out of here?"

"Are you asking me if I'm poaching deer or if I killed Trace Winchester?" Buzz demanded, then slammed his palms against the bars, before turning his back to Luke. "Just get me out of here."

MCCALL SHOWERED AND DRESSED after Luke left, feeling bereft and edgy. She thought of their lovemaking and ached to be back in his arms. She'd once thought she couldn't live without him. She'd been seventeen then. The ten years apart had been hell.

But this was worse. Last night proved how they felt about each other. They were in love, had been for years. They'd come together again in the most intimate of ways, the passion blinding, the aching need to be together almost more than either of them could stand. Nothing should have been able to drive them apart.

But it had.

She'd seen how torn Luke had been between his loyalty to the uncle who'd raised him and the woman he loved. Before, his cousin had come between them. Now it was his uncle.

Whatever the old feud between the two families, it was still going strong. Why couldn't Luke see that his uncle was guilty? Because he was too close to it.

Or was she the one who was too close to see the truth?

McCall shook her head. All the evidence pointed to Buzz. He was the one who'd caught Trace poaching, and yet as much as he'd harassed her father, Buzz had sworn he hadn't taken the rifle. A red flag.

Then finding the pickup in the Crawford stock pond. Buzz would have known that the place was vacant, no one around for miles to see him get rid of the truck and hike back to the ridge. The walk back to his own vehicle wouldn't have been that tough for a man who walked hundreds of miles a year as a game warden.

Finding the rifle at his house was just the icing on the cake. The only other evidence that could put the nail in Buzz Crawford's coffin was the pages from his daily log for the days in question.

Would the sheriff have thought to check them?

She couldn't depend on Luke to help her now, she realized. When it came to loyalties, blood was always thicker than water. Luke would stand by his uncle.

When her cell phone rang, McCall hoped it was Luke. It wasn't. Nor was it her mother, who would have been her second guess. Ruby would be furious that McCall hadn't called to give her the news before everyone else in town heard about Buzz's arrest.

To McCall's surprise, it was her grandmother.

"I need to see you," Pepper Winchester said. "Can you come out here now?"

"Only if you promise not to call the sheriff this time."

A slight hesitation, then, "I apologize for that. I would appreciate it if you would drive out to the ranch. It's important or I wouldn't ask. I will have Enid make us lunch."

"You sure she won't try to poison me?" McCall asked, only half joking.

"We could make her taste it, if you like." Pepper sounded serious.

She tried not to take this invitation for more than it was. Her mother was right: she would be a fool to think that anything had changed with her grandmother. Pepper wanted something from her. The only question was what?

But going out to her grandmother's for lunch was better than sitting around hoping Luke would come back.

"Okay. I'll see you soon."

McCall couldn't help being anxious though as she drove out to the Winchester Ranch. Another spring thunderstorm had blown in and she had to shift into four-wheel drive to get down the muddy road.

She worried about ending up in a ditch again, only this time no Luke to save her since she hadn't thought to tell anyone where she'd gone.

Just the thought of Luke made her want to cry. She felt strung too tight and knew she couldn't trust her emotions.

She was tired, drained emotionally, physically and mentally. Of course she would feel this way after finding out that her father had been murdered.

That was what made her feel vulnerable and scared. Not falling for Luke all over again. She hated feeling this way. Why had she opened herself up to this again?

She knew that since finding her father's grave and realizing he'd been murdered, it hadn't really sunk in. She'd put the pieces together, found the pickup, and everything had quickly—too quickly—fallen into place after that because of the rifle. Because Buzz didn't have the sense to dump it.

Criminals were notoriously stupid. It was why so many of them got caught. Why crime didn't pay.

She realized what was bothering her. She didn't know why Buzz had killed her father. Blackmail? Blackmailers tended to get killed for obvious reasons—

death being the only way to keep the bloodsucking leeches off you permanently.

What had Buzz done that Trace Winchester had found out about?

Or maybe it hadn't been blackmail. Maybe Buzz had just lost his temper with Trace. Clearly, from all the tickets he'd written Trace, he had it in for him. So who knew what had happened on that ridge.

As McCall pulled up in front of the Winchester Ranch lodge, the old blue heeler came out to growl and a curtain moved behind a window at the end of one wing.

McCall got out and, again keeping an eye on the dog, went to the door and knocked.

This time it was her grandmother who answered. Her long thick hair was freshly plaited. She wore black just as she had on the first visit, but she'd added a beautiful gold link necklace.

She looked graceful and elegant, and McCall couldn't help but notice that her expression seemed softer.

"Thank you for coming on such short notice," Pepper said. She motioned McCall into the parlor again, but this time there was a fire going in the fireplace, a welcome addition on a day like this.

McCall took the chair she was offered, noticing the scrapbooks on the coffee table in front of her.

"I have something I thought you'd like to see before lunch," her grandmother said, taking a chair next to her and opening one of the books.

McCall saw at once that the scrapbooks were filled with family photographs. Her heart leaped in her chest at the sight of four children beside Pepper, who looked young and beautiful. She was holding the baby, Trace.

The four young children were her Aunt Virginia and Uncles Angus, Brand and Worth. This was the first time she'd laid eyes on them. As far as she knew, none of them had returned to the ranch after Trace disappeared. Apparently she had cousins she'd never met, as well.

Worry as to why her grandmother was showing her these put a damper on her excitement at this glimpse into her family and her father's earlier life.

"Your father was the sweetest baby," Pepper said, touching the baby's face in the photo. She turned a page. "He was two here."

McCall stared at the photo of her father. "He was adorable."

Her grandmother smiled. "Yes, he was. I spoiled him—I know that." She turned the page, pointing out Trace in each photograph even though it wasn't necessary.

He was the handsomest of Pepper's children and clearly her favorite. She noticed what could have been jealousy in the faces of the others in one photo where Pepper was making a fuss over Trace. McCall felt a growing unease.

"Trace was such a good boy. A little wild like his father, but he had a good, strong heart." Pepper's voice broke with emotion, and she turned her face aside to wipe furtively at her tears.

McCall touched a finger to the photo of her father as a boy, seeing herself in the squint of his eyes, the cocky stance, the dark straight hair and high cheekbones.

Pepper turned the page, and McCall smiled when she saw the snapshots of her father as a teenager. It was clear why Ruby had fallen so hard for him. He was stunningly handsome, a mischievous look in his dark eyes, a swagger about him.

"He was so good-looking," McCall said, almost lamenting the fact, given what Red had told her about her father and women.

"He played football the year they went to state," Pepper said. "He was quite the athlete, but his first love was hunting."

She looked up then. "I heard you were the one who found his truck."

"It was a lucky guess," McCall said, uncomfortable with her grandmother's intense gaze on her.

"He loved that truck. I ordered it special for him. It looks nothing now like the pickup my son drove away in the last time I saw him." She cleared her throat. "I had wondered what happened to his rifle. It was his grandfather's, you know. An old model 99 Savage. It had his grandfather's and father's initials carved in the stock. How foolish of the killer to keep it, don't you think?"

It was the first she'd spoken of her son's death and Buzz Crawford's arrest. Something in her words filled McCall with a growing uneasiness.

A bell tinkled down the hall. Her grandmother closed the scrapbook and rose. Was it possible Pepper didn't believe Buzz had killed her son?

But why?

EUGENE DIDN'T SHOW UP for the bail hearing, much to Luke's relief. It was just as well, since he wasn't sure what he might do to Eugene when he saw him. That thought filled him with a hollow sadness. And to think he'd felt as if Eugene was like a brother to him—like Abel and Cain as it turned out.

The judge set bail for five hundred thousand, saying

he didn't believe Buzz, who had served the county for years as a game warden, was a flight risk.

Luke put up his land to raise the money to get his uncle out on bail, then got in his pickup and headed for Glasgow and the game warden district office where all daily logs were kept—including those stored from Buzz's time as warden.

He told himself he was doing this for McCall. In truth, he would have done anything for her, not that she would believe it right now. He knew from the look on her face this morning that she thought he'd chosen his family over her.

She was wrong about that.

But he was going to Glasgow for himself as much as McCall. He needed to know the truth, and he hoped it could be found in what Buzz had written in his daily logs.

A tumbleweed cartwheeled across the road propelled by a wind that lay over the grass and howled at the windows of the pickup. Luke could see another spring thunderstorm moving across the prairie toward him.

He loved the storms in this part of the country. Everything was intense up here, from the weather to the light that made the pale green spring grasses glow and warmed the Larb Hills in the distance to a dusty purple.

The storm swept across the open landscape, rain pelting the pickup, wind chasing tumbleweeds to trap them in the barbed wire fences that lined the two-lane.

As the rain passed, Luke rolled down his window and breathed in the smell of spring. The storm had left the land looking even greener, the sky washed a pale blue.

He wished McCall was with him right now, knowing she would appreciate this scene. He hadn't been able to get her out of his head. But that was nothing new. Last night, though, had only made him want her more after wanting this woman most of his adult life. Now they had a chance. Or they had had one before his uncle called.

While Luke had made his choice when he'd decided to do this, he still felt disloyal as he entered the Glasgow FWP regional office.

It surprised him that McCall believed Buzz was a killer but that Buzz wouldn't lie about where he'd been in his warden's daily log. Was his uncle really that arrogant—and that foolish?

Twenty-seven years ago in the fall, Buzz would have probably been down in the Missouri Breaks at the far south of his jurisdiction for most of the day checking on bow elk hunters. He would be needed there more than out in the prairie looking for a possible antelope poacher.

Except, even if that's what Buzz had done, he would still have had to drive right past the road to the ridge where Trace Winchester's body had been buried. Right past the old Crawford place where Trace's pickup had been sunk in the mud at the bottom of the stock pond.

Buzz could have killed Trace Winchester, buried him on the ridge and gotten rid of his pickup in the pond.

But Luke didn't believe he had. Or maybe he just didn't want to believe Buzz would commit murder.

"Mornin' Helen," Luke said as he recognized the older woman working the main desk.

"Hi, Luke. What brings you to the big city?" she joked. "I didn't see a trial on the schedule."

"Nope, not today. I'm on another errand. I need to

know where I can find the game warden daily logs from twenty-seven years ago." He knew they kept them in case a legal problem came up years down the road.

"Twenty-seven years ago? Those would be in our storage facility at the other end of town. I can give you the key. They're all filed by month and year. Do you know what date you're looking for?"

He nodded. "Shouldn't take me long."

"HOW IS YOUR LUNCH? Poison-free?" Pepper Winchester actually smiled, her dark eyes almost teasing.

"Fine," McCall said, a lie. Enid was no cook. Still, that wasn't the only reason she'd lost her appetite, she thought as she put down her fork. "Why did you really invite me out here? It wasn't for lunch or photos."

Her grandmother arched a brow as she put down her fork and pushed away her nearly untouched lunch. "Why did Buzz Crawford kill my son?"

"I beg your pardon?" McCall was taken aback by the abruptness of the question.

Pepper's direct gaze bored into her. "There must have been a reason."

McCall had asked herself the same question. "I don't know. I suppose it will come out in the trial."

Her grandmother looked skeptical. "Let's hope so. If you hear anything, you'll let me know?"

McCall nodded and was about to tell her grandmother that she'd been suspended and wouldn't be hearing much.

But Pepper stood, signaling lunch and the visit were over. As she turned to leave, she said over her shoulder, "You know the way out?"

Before McCall could answer, her grandmother had disappeared back into the gloom and doom of the old lodge.

But from the shadows, McCall caught a glimpse of Enid before the housekeeper ducked out of sight.

THE DOOR TO THE METAL storage unit opened with a groan. A blast of musty hot air hit Luke in the face as he reached in to turn on the light.

The long narrow building was filled with shelves from floor to ceiling, the ones closest to the door, the most recent. He entered the maze of shelves and worked his way to those from twenty-seven years ago.

According to McCall, Buzz had caught Trace Winchester poaching an antelope before the opening of antelope season. That could have meant minutes before daylight. Or the night before.

Luke pulled down the logbook for October and, stepping under one of the bare bulb lights, flipped through the book.

The notes were all written in his uncle's precise printing—until he got to the day in question. The first entry on October 20 was of Trace Winchester's poaching violation. But what had Luke's heart racing was that the entry was nearly illegible. The words ran together, looking hurriedly scrawled.

And not just that, Luke realized. The entry was written in black ink—while all the rest of the entries and those after that day were in blue.

It was a small thing and if he hadn't known Buzz the way he did, he wouldn't have thought anything of it. Buzz prided himself on doing everything neat and tidy and by the book.

Buzz had broken with routine, indicating he'd been upset and hurried.

According to his uncle's notation, he'd gotten a call from dispatch asking him to check on a possible problem on the ridge where Trace Winchester's remains had been found.

He'd responded, found Trace poaching an antelope, written him a ticket. He'd made no mention of Trace's rifle.

Luke stared at the writing until it blurred before his eyes, feeling sick. Buzz had been there and might be the only person still alive who knew what happened on that ridge that day.

Chapter Fourteen

News that Buzz Crawford had been released from jail hit the streets at the speed of light. McCall heard it at the first stop she made once back in Whitehorse after her lunch with her grandmother.

She got the feeling that everyone had believed him guilty and if not guilty, then at least *capable* of murder.

The sheriff caught her as she was coming out of the post office.

"McCall?" Grant was standing beside her car, clearly waiting for her. She thought about seeing him parked down the street from his house and wondered again if he'd been spying on her—or his wife.

"Sheriff." Had her grandmother called him about her again?

"I just wanted to let you know that Buzz Crawford is out on bail."

She wondered why he hadn't just called her. Maybe he had. She hadn't checked her messages since she feared there wouldn't be one from Luke.

"I heard," she said. "It's all anyone in town is talking about."

"Sorry I didn't let you know sooner. Luke got him out on bail."

Good ol' Luke.

The sheriff seemed to hesitate. "I also wanted to let you know that Buzz filed a formal complaint against you, saying he believes you planted the rifle in his house in an attempt to frame him. I know that isn't the case," Grant said quickly. "But he's pretty worked up. If he should come by your place, just call the department at once."

"Sure." And twenty minutes later someone would arrive at her cabin twenty minutes too late?

"Eugene got himself locked up last night," the sheriff said. "Drunk and disorderly. He hasn't made bail."

"At least Luke didn't get him out," she said, more to herself than the sheriff.

"Just watch your back." The sheriff cleared his throat. "I never thanked you for your work in finding the pickup. I'm sorry I had to take you off the case. And I wouldn't worry too much about Buzz. He's too smart to threaten you. He's in enough trouble as it is."

She wished she could be that sure of what Buzz Crawford would do. Or had done, for that matter.

WHEN LUKE RETURNED to the cabin, he found McCall standing at the edge of the deck looking over the river. She had a blanket wrapped around her shoulders and a beer in her hand.

She turned at the sound of his footfalls and he saw her expression. She hadn't been sure he would return.

"What are you doing out here?" he asked.

"Enjoying the evening." He saw she had the gun he'd

given her tucked into the waistband of her jeans and wondered if she wasn't out here because she could hear anyone who approached. Obviously she'd heard that Buzz had been released from jail.

Luke had stopped by the lake house but hadn't found Buzz at home. He wasn't sure what he planned to say to his uncle. He wasn't sure what there was to say. He ended up leaving a note:

> Buzz,
> We need to talk,
> Luke

He knew it sounded cryptic, but he also didn't want to leave anything that could be potentially incriminating. Telling Buzz about what he'd found in the logbook would have been.

After he'd left Buzz's place, all he'd wanted to do was return to McCall.

Now, without a word, he stepped to her and took her in his arms. He didn't want to talk about anything, especially his uncle. He wasn't going to let anything come between them ever again.

"I checked Buzz's logbook," he said, drawing back to look into her eyes. "You were right. The evidence is there. As I was leaving, the sheriff arrived. He took the book."

She nodded, not seeming surprised. "I'm sorry."

"Me, too."

She motioned to the cooler at her feet. "You look like you could use a beer."

He smiled and let go of her long enough to take a beer from the box and unscrew the top. He pulled on the beer, taking a long drink. She was right. This was exactly what he needed, something cold to drink, a nice view and the woman he loved.

Dark shadows were forming in the river bottom as another short spring day turned to dusk. He could hear a flock of geese honking softly from the shallows. A breeze stirred McCall's dark hair. He breathed in her scent as he snuggled against her back and slipped a hand inside her shirt to cup her bare breast.

Desire sparked along his nerve endings, firing that old familiar need in him. The passion had been there the first time they'd touched and nothing had dampened it, not even the years spent apart.

She turned to kiss him, tasting of cold beer. He dragged her to him, encircling her with his arms, deepening the kiss. Her body molded to his, and he could feel the frantic beat of her heart.

"Unless you want me to make love to you right here on this deck, I think we'd better go inside," he whispered as he drew back from the kiss.

She smiled up at him and whispered back, "What is wrong with out here on the deck?"

IT WASN'T UNTIL LATER, snuggled together under the blanket, their clothing pillowed beneath their heads and the starry night above, that they heard the sirens.

McCall sat up as she saw the flashing lights and saw where they were headed—toward the lake. "Luke?"

She'd barely gotten the word out before he was up and pulling on his clothing.

"I have a bad feeling," he said.

She had one as well as she quickly dressed and they took his pickup and headed north, following the lights of the sheriff and ambulance.

As they turned off the road, McCall saw what she'd feared. Both the patrol car and the ambulance had stopped in front of Buzz's house.

Luke pulled up in the pickup and jumped out. As he ran toward the house, McCall saw a deputy stop him. She turned to look for the sheriff and, spotting him, hurried over.

"What's happened?" she asked.

"Buzz committed suicide."

"Suicide?" She couldn't help sounding astonished. Buzz Crawford was the least likely person she knew to even contemplate suicide. "Are you sure?"

"He left a note," Grant said. "He's the one who killed your father, McCall. He confessed. I guess, confronted with all the evidence…"

She nodded, thinking about what Luke had said he'd found in Buzz's logbook. Still, she felt shaken. Buzz had taken the cowardly way out, and while her heart ached for Luke and his loss, she was angry that she and her mother hadn't gotten to see this go to trial. This didn't feel like closure because now they would never know why.

She turned to see Luke, his face twisted in anguish as he came toward them.

"They won't let me in," he said to the sheriff. "They said he's dead?"

"I'm sorry, Luke. Buzz shot himself. He left a suicide note along with a confession to the killing of Trace Winchester."

LUKE DROVE MCCALL BACK to her cabin, too stunned and distraught to talk and thankful she didn't question him.

"I need to be the one to tell Eugene," he said as he pulled up next to her cabin. He leaned in, kissed her and said, "I'm sorry about your dad. You tried to warn me."

"I'm sorry, too," she said and, touching his cheek, told him to be careful before she got out of the truck.

"I need some time," he said. "I might go out to my place at least to check things tonight. But I'll see you tomorrow, okay?"

She smiled in understanding. "Don't worry about me. Take all the time you need. I know you'll be back." She closed the door and walked toward her cabin.

He waited until she was inside before he turned around and drove through the darkness, feeling as if he'd been hit by a train.

His mind was racing. He'd found what could constitute evidence in Buzz's logbook. Had the sheriff shown it to Buzz? Is that why his uncle had decided to write the confession and kill himself?

Luke drove toward town, turning it all over in his head. The night was black. No stars, no moon, the clouds so low now it was like driving through cotton. He had his side window down letting the cold night air blow in.

He didn't feel the chill, only the intense sense of loss and regret. He kept rehashing his last conversation with Buzz over in his head and blaming himself that he hadn't seen this coming.

Didn't everyone say there were signs? Buzz had been acting strangely, but Luke had thought he was just bored with retirement and worried about Eugene.

Luke had never believed that a man like Buzz would

ever do something like this. Murder? Then suicide? He had a bad feeling that the ones least likely to commit either were the ones who would surprise you.

For Buzz it might have been a case of the perfect storm: the arrest, his disappointment in Eugene. Suspecting, as Luke did, that Eugene had been using his pickup to poach could have been the last straw.

A thought crossed his mind. He scoffed at the idea but couldn't shake a nagging feeling that the thought hadn't been as crazy as he wanted to believe.

Luke slowed the pickup on the edge of Whitehorse and headed for the sheriff's department—and the county jail where his cousin was still locked up the last he'd heard.

MCCALL FELT NUMB AS SHE stopped on the deck to pick up the blanket she'd left there. The darkness seemed to close in along with the shock.

Buzz was dead.

She wrapped the blanket around herself and stood staring down at the river through the deep black of cottonwoods. No starlight filtered past the bare branches. No moon shone in Montana's big sky.

The only light was a ghostly glaze that shimmered on the surface of the water as it snaked past.

McCall shivered and pulled the blanket tighter as a gust of wind moaned through the trees.

It was over.

Buzz had killed her father, and while she would never know why, at least she should be thankful that Trace Winchester had gotten justice.

So why did she feel so empty, she wondered as she

leaned against the railing and breathed in the rich scents from the river bottom. It was over.

Over for some, she thought. Not for Luke, though.

Suddenly she felt as if icy fingers had brushed across the back of her neck. Her stomach contracted with a feeling she was no longer alone, and that what was waiting for her in the dark wasn't just dangerous—it was deadly.

She stared hard into the black cottonwoods, listening for any hint that there was someone out there watching her at this very moment. Eugene? Had he gotten out of jail? The wind moaned through the branches, the limbs moving restlessly against the dark sky.

Taking a step back, she edged toward the front door of the house, trying to remember if she'd locked it, suddenly filled with a sense of dread.

She'd only taken a few steps when she remembered the gun Luke had given her. She'd had it earlier on the deck...

She stopped, her gaze scanning the dark shadows of the deck. She couldn't see it. Maybe Luke had picked it up. Or maybe they had knocked it off the deck earlier.

As badly as she wished she could find it, she wasn't about to take the time to look for it. Turning, she lunged for her front door, that feeling of danger too intense to ignore.

The knob turned in her hand. She hadn't locked it. Damn.

She stepped in, fumbling for the light as she slammed the door behind her, breathing hard.

There's no one out there. You're just spooked over everything that has happened. You're running scared and it's not like you.

McCall reached for the lock but froze. Had it been the soft scuff of a shoe? Or a breath exhaled? Or had she just sensed it as she had on the deck?

Whatever the reason, even before McCall hit the light switch and spun around, she knew. Someone was behind her.

"WHAT ARE YOU DOING HERE?" Eugene said from his cell bunk when Luke walked in. "You'd better be here to get me out. Because if you've come to give me a lecture…"

Luke gripped the bars. Obviously no one had told him about Buzz yet. "I need to know something, Eugene. I told Buzz that someone was using his pickup to poach deer along the river."

His cousin leaned back on his bunk. "When did you tell him that?"

Luke swallowed back his guilt. "Right before he was released from jail."

"And let me guess. You suspect I was using the pickup. What was I doing with the deer?"

"Selling them to a client in Billings to pay for your gambling debts."

To his surprise, Eugene began to laugh. "Doesn't that sound a little too organized for a worthless ne'er-do-well like me?" his cousin asked, getting up and coming over to the bars. "Huh, hotshot game warden?"

"What are you trying to tell me?" Luke asked, afraid he already knew what was coming.

"Buzz. It was *his* idea. He was bored and if anyone knew how to poach and get away with it, it was Buzz. Why do you think we went to Billings? To unload what we'd killed." He laughed again. "Don't look so shocked.

Buzz used to poach all the time when he was warden. You didn't notice how our meat supply never ran low?"

Luke stared at his cousin, remembering what McCall had said about her mother thinking Trace might have had something on Buzz he was using as leverage. "Did Buzz also mention that Trace Winchester was blackmailing him?"

Eugene grinned. "Well, if Trace was, I can tell you this much—no one blackmails Buzz for long." His cousin shook his head, giving Luke a disgusted look. "You always thought you were better than us, didn't you? Buzz joked that as great as you thought you were, you'd never catch us. Even if you did, Buzz said you'd never arrest us." He turned to go back to his cot. "When you see Buzz, tell him to spring me from the joint."

"I'm afraid Buzz isn't going to be springing anyone," Luke said. "He committed suicide tonight after confessing to killing Trace Winchester."

"PLEASE DON'T DO ANYTHING heroic," Sandy said, rising from the kitchen chair where she'd been sitting, waiting.

Heart hammering, McCall heard the click of the safety being flipped off on the pistol as she stared at Sandy Sheridan. Two thoughts zipped past. What was the sheriff's wife doing here pointing a gun at her? And Luke wouldn't be back tonight.

"How *did* you get the job with my husband?" Sandy asked as she advanced on her, the gun steady in her hand and pointed at McCall's heart. "Because you aren't afraid of anything? Or was it because you could twist Grant around your little finger? He always told me how much he liked you."

From the expression on Sandy's face, that had been a mistake on the sheriff's part.

"What are you doing here?" McCall asked, understanding only that she was in serious trouble. That over-caffeinated, frantic look was in Sandy's eyes, and she held the gun like a woman who knew how to use it.

Sandy gave her an impatient look. "Don't try to con me. The moment I saw you standing at my front door, I knew that Grant was right. He said you made a damned good deputy because you were bright and saw what other people didn't."

"You're both giving me too much credit," McCall said. Outside, the wind had picked up. It whipped the cottonwoods, a limb scraping against the side of the house and flickering shadows past the window. "I haven't a clue why you're here."

"Guess," Sandy said with a giggle.

A thought worked its way through the panic. "Buzz didn't kill my father."

Sandy laughed, a sound like piano wires snapping. "How can you say that? The man confessed."

No doubt at gunpoint.

McCall tried to concentrate, but the wind and trees whipping against the cabin kept distracting her. She felt too tired for this, her mind numb from shock and fear and a deep sense of regret.

How could she have been so wrong? Buzz had looked so guilty, *too* guilty. No wonder she'd felt such an emptiness when it had looked as if he'd done it—and taken the easy way out.

The sheriff was right: she *had* been too emotionally involved.

"You aren't going to tell me *you* killed my father, are you?" McCall asked. "I thought you loved him." She was only a few feet away from Sandy, but she knew better than to make a play for the gun.

"I *did* love him." Hatred flared in Sandy's eyes. "I *loved* him more than you can ever understand. I would have done anything for him. And what did he do to me? He broke my heart." She was crying now but still holding the gun aimed at McCall's heart.

McCall's mind was racing again as she tried to put it all together. "Trace felt guilty about what he'd done to you, so of course he would agree to meet you on the ridge to talk."

Sandy's eyes narrowed. "Very good."

Trace had been furious with Ruby over her little tryst with Red, so he would have been primed to do anything his old girlfriend asked.

"But things got out of hand," McCall guessed.

"He refused to leave that tramp and you," Sandy said. "I told him you probably weren't even his baby. He thought he was just going to get to walk away from me." Her eyes took on a faraway look that turned McCall's blood to slush.

Outside the cabin, something moved across the window. Not a limb. *Someone.*

"So you killed him," McCall said, trying hard not to look past Sandy to the window again. Someone was out there headed for the front door. Luke? But he'd said he wouldn't be back. Her heart soared then dropped like a stone. Had he seen the sheriff's wife holding the gun on her? If he hadn't, he'd be walking into this deadly situation.

"What did you use? A gun, a knife, a rock?" McCall asked as she took a couple of steps toward the back of the cabin, hoping to turn Sandy so she wouldn't be able to see whoever was about to open the front door.

"What are you doing?" Sandy demanded, grabbing the weapon with both hands. "Stop moving."

"I just need to sit down," McCall said, motioning toward the kitchen chair nearby.

"You'll be lying down soon enough and for a very long time," Sandy snapped. "Enjoy standing."

"So how did you do it?" McCall asked, forced to be content with having turned Sandy at least most of the way from the door.

"I shot him if you must know."

"With the same gun you're holding on me?" McCall asked.

"As a matter of fact. Ironic, isn't it?"

The front door eased open. McCall still couldn't see who it was, but the way it opened, she was sure the person outside had seen what was going on.

"Then you buried him on the ridge," McCall said. "Took his rifle—"

"Don't be ridiculous. I left as quickly as I could, but as we were driving back to town, I passed Game Warden Buzz Crawford and remembered the vendetta he and Trace had going on. I put in a call to Fish and Game saying there was someone poaching on the ridge. I knew once Buzz found Trace dead, he wouldn't call it in. He knew no one would believe him, not the way he hounded Trace all the time. Everyone would believe he did it."

Something Sandy said stopped McCall for a moment, but she couldn't put her finger on what it was before Sandy finished. McCall could imagine Buzz finding Trace's body. He would know he'd been set up. The smart thing would have been for him to call 911, but Sandy was right. He would have looked guilty no matter what. He had motive and opportunity, and he was standing over his nemesis's dead body.

It explained why Buzz had acted so guilty. Everything was starting to make sense. "Buzz buried Trace and got rid of the pickup in the stock pond, then wrote up a poaching ticket to make it look as if my father skipped town because of it."

Sandy smiled, clearly pleased with herself.

Out of the corner of her eye, McCall saw a blurred dark shape slip in through the front door and drop behind the couch. "And you took my father's rifle."

"I thought I might need it someday. As it turned out, I did. Grant was forever boring me to death with talk about his cases. It was too easy to know exactly when to plant the rifle and make sure Buzz Crawford took the fall."

"Nice job," McCall said, horrified and yet at the same time awed by Sandy's twisted criminal mind. "But Buzz must have wondered who the real killer was." The answer came to her in a flash. "My mother."

That would explain why Buzz hated Ruby Bates Winchester so much. He thought she'd killed Trace and framed him for the murder. That's why he'd thought McCall had access to Trace's rifle and had used it to frame him.

"Bingo!" Sandy said with an unhinged glee.

"You tied it all up with a nice big bow on top," McCall said. "If you'd just left it at that, you would probably have gotten away with it. But once you murder me, you will ruin your perfect scheme."

"Oh, that's just it. I'm not quite done yet. But I will be after you write your confession, admitting that in an attempt to protect your mother, you framed Buzz and, racked with guilt, took your own life."

"You really don't think anyone is going to believe my mother killed Trace or that I framed Buzz, do you?"

Sandy burst out laughing. "Are you serious? Everyone in town has speculated for years that Ruby did it. And all of Whitehorse has questioned having a woman deputy in the sheriff's department. Everyone knows we're the weaker sex," she added with a chortle. "It will break poor Grant's heart since he is so fond of you. But that's the price he pays for hiring you in the first place."

The dark shape rose behind Sandy, and with a start, McCall saw the man's face. Sheriff Grant Sheridan?

That's when McCall remembered what Sandy had said that had caught her attention. *We.* She'd said "*we*" were driving back to town" after murdering Trace.

Sandy hadn't been alone that day when she'd met McCall's father on the ridge.

McCall's gaze shot to Grant. The sheriff was out of uniform, dressed in a faded long-sleeved shirt, a pair of worn jeans and sneakers. His head was bare. He stood, arms akimbo, his usually forlorn face set in deep ridges of disappointment.

He stood behind Sandy, his weapon drawn—but pointed at the floor.

LUKE HAD STARTED DOWN Highway 191 toward his place south of town when he'd passed, first Sandy Sheridan, then moments later, the sheriff.

Grant was driving his old pickup instead of his patrol car, and he wore a baseball cap pulled low.

Luke wasn't sure what had made him curious as he'd watched Grant in his rearview mirror. The sheriff pulled over, leaving his motor running, as if to let a car go by before he fell in behind his wife again.

He's following her, Luke thought, as Sandy turned down the river road—and Grant followed a good distance behind.

Luke swung his rig around and went after them, wondering if something else had happened. Since his talk with Eugene, he'd been so upset he hadn't been thinking clearly.

But now as he came around a curve in the road, he saw that Sandy had pulled off at the fishing access closest to McCall's cabin on the river. If there was one thing Luke knew, it was that Sandy Sheridan was no fisherman.

Even stranger, the sheriff made a quick turn onto a ranch road, going only a short distance before pulling into the trees and cutting his lights.

Luke kept going on past the ranch turnoff and the fishing access road. As soon as he knew he was out of sight around a curve, he pulled over, cutting his lights and engine and got out.

He waited a moment for his eyes to adjust to the darkness, then he headed back down the road toward McCall's cabin, working his way through the trees. Ahead, he saw a dark figure come out of the trees from the spot where Grant had parked his pickup.

What the hell was going on? Whatever it was, it couldn't have anything to do with McCall, right?

Then how did he explain why the sheriff's wife appeared to be headed right for the cabin?

Luke had to hang back to let the sheriff cross the road and disappear into the trees, before he continued to follow the two.

He lost sight of Sandy near McCall's cabin. A moment later he saw the sheriff sneaking along the side of the cabin, then disappearing around to the deck door.

Luke followed, his anxiety growing. When he heard the first shot, he took off at a run. Earlier, during their lovemaking, he'd remembered seeing the pistol he'd lent McCall beside a flowerpot on the deck.

McCALL STARED AT GRANT, realizing he must have been the person Sandy was with that day. It seemed odd, but who else could it have been?

Grant hadn't moved. He stood with his head down, looking sick, his weapon still dangling from his right hand.

Sandy still hadn't realized they weren't alone. "Your mother ruined my life when you took Trace away from me," Sandy said. "He wouldn't have left—if Ruby hadn't been pregnant with *you*."

McCall saw where this was going. And if Sandy and Grant had killed Trace—

The front door blew open. Grant apparently hadn't closed it properly.

Sandy swung around and saw her husband, Grant. Her finger must have been itching on the trigger because she got off the first shot.

McCall heard the second shot as she dived for the door. A bloodcurdling scream followed the report of the gunfire. Someone groaned.

As McCall scrambled toward the front door, she saw Grant trying to get to his feet. He still had the gun in his hand. Was it possible he'd shot Sandy? Or had he been trying to hit McCall?

"Stop!" Sandy yelled. "I don't want to shoot you in the back, but I will."

The third bullet ricocheted off the wall next to McCall, sending splinters into the air. McCall stopped and lifted her hands as she slowly turned around to face Sandy.

Grant, she saw, had fallen back on the floor, facedown in his own blood. Sandy had his gun—and her own. Blood bloomed from her left side, but she seemed oblivious of being hit. Grant had shot her? To shut her up? Or keep her from killing McCall?

McCall glanced at Grant, watching for any sign of life. None. Meeting Sandy's gaze, she prepared herself to meet her maker. Sandy had nothing to lose now.

She had killed Grant. Now she had to kill McCall.

There would be no suicide note. No pretend suicide.

"It's over, Sandy," McCall said, knowing her only chance was to try to talk the woman down. "The killing has to stop. Trace is dead. Now Grant. I don't know what happened on that ridge all those years ago with my father, but I do know that you didn't mean to shoot Grant and I don't believe you would have killed Trace if it hadn't been for Grant being on that ridge with you that day."

Sandy began to laugh. "You aren't as smart as Grant thought you were. Grant wasn't with me when I killed Trace."

"Then who…"

"I wasn't the only one who hated Trace." Sandy spat out the words. "It wasn't even my idea to get him on that ridge in sight of the Winchester ranch." She smiled at McCall's shock. "They say blood is thicker than water." Sandy shook her head. "Not when it comes to sibling rivalry. Trace's own flesh and blood wanted him dead. What does that say about your father?"

"You're lying."

"How different it would have been if Trace had married me," Sandy said. "He would have changed," she said with conviction, showing just how delusional she was.

For a moment, Sandy seemed to be lost in a daydream of what her life could have been like if she'd been the one to get Trace Winchester down the aisle. Her face softened as she steadied the gun with both hands to kill McCall, her eyes moist, a smile on her lips as if seeing herself beside Trace in the small white chapel on the edge of town.

That's how she died.

McCall would later wonder if Sandy even felt the bullet that pierced her heart. Luke's shot had been true. He'd fired at the same time he'd thrown McCall to the side. Sandy's shot had burrowed into McCall's front door in the exact spot where she'd been standing just an instant before.

It had been so close that she swore she felt it brush past. Luke had saved her life.

The realization came with tears as she'd looked over at him, the two of them lying on her living room floor. He'd mouthed the words. Or at least she thought he had, since the sound of the gunshot so close to her ear had made her think she'd gone deaf.

I love you.

And then she was in his arms, and he was holding her as if he would never let her go ever again.

Epilogue

There is nothing the community of Whitehorse loved more than a scandal—unless it was a scandal followed by talk of a wedding.

It took no time at all for everyone in the county and beyond to hear about what happened at Deputy Sheriff McCall Winchester's cabin on the river.

Both McCall and Luke were considered heroes. It became clear that a lot of people hadn't liked Sandy Sheridan, especially after it came out that she'd been running around with their husbands behind Grant's back.

McCall had figured that was how Grant had ended up at her cabin. He'd been following Sandy, just as he'd been the other time she'd seen him, and was presumably aware of her transgressions. It was too bad, because McCall realized after the dust settled that Grant had loved Sandy or he would have killed her that night in the cabin—and not just wounded her.

How ironic that Sandy had passed up true love for what she thought she could have had with Trace Winchester.

The whole episode had shaken a lot of people, including McCall's mother.

"I think I'm in love with Red," Ruby had said a few days later. "Don't worry. I'm going to take it slow. I just wanted you to know."

McCall had been touched and had hugged her mother, hoping that she had finally found a man who would do her right. If anyone could be that man, it was Red Harper.

Ruby wasn't the only one who'd been shaken by what had happened. When Luke had asked McCall to ride with him out to the house he was building, she'd been happy to go along.

He'd walked her through it, explaining what he'd planned in each room, and she saw at once that the house he'd been building was too large for one person.

"You were building this for us," she said on a shaky breath.

He smiled, and she thought that he had to be the most handsome man in the world. Her heart began to beat faster as he reached in his pocket and, shoving back his cowboy hat, dropped to one knee.

"McCall Winchester, will you marry me?"

She'd been afraid of love since she was old enough to understand that her own father had run out on her and her pregnant mother. Falling for Luke at such a young age—and thinking he'd betrayed her—had made her more than a little gun-shy.

But when she looked into his eyes and saw the love, McCall knew there was only one thing she could say.

"Yes. Oh yes!" And she'd thrown herself into his arms, ready for whatever the future held.

She hadn't been so sure about staying on at the sheriff's department. Former sheriff Carter Jackson stepped in to help after Grant's death and had asked her to stop by. He offered to reinstate her whenever she was ready to come back.

"I'm not sure I can come back as a deputy." But not for the reasons the sheriff was probably thinking. It wasn't her brush with death. It was not knowing for sure who'd been on that ridge the day her father had died.

With Sandy, Grant and Buzz all dead, she knew she might never know. She didn't want to spend her life chasing after a killer. So what kind of deputy did that make her?

"Why don't you give it some time," Carter was saying. "Don't make a decision now."

Because she wasn't her father, she nodded and said she would.

As she walked out of the sheriff's department, she was asking herself, what now? when her grandmother called and asked to see her.

"Why?" McCall asked.

The question seemed to take Pepper aback for a moment. "Must you always be so difficult?"

Diplomacy kept McCall from answering that one.

"Isn't it possible I just want to see you, perhaps congratulate you on your engagement?"

McCall drove out to the ranch, wondering if she could trust this change in her grandmother.

Maybe Pepper had found peace now that she believed Trace's killer was dead. McCall had no intention of ever telling her any different.

McCall wanted to believe that Sandy had lied. Either way she knew what that would do to Pepper. She'd lost her family twenty-seven years ago.

Recently her grandmother had mentioned contacting her family and inviting them for a visit at the ranch.

The deputy in McCall noted that such a visit would mean the suspects would be back on the ranch.

"So when is the wedding?" her grandmother asked now on the other end of the phone.

"Christmas."

"That's a wonderful time for a wedding."

A little worried about why her grandmother wanted to see her, McCall said she was on her way and hung up.

Pepper opened the door at her knock, thanked her for coming and ushered McCall into the parlor.

"Would you like something to drink? I could have Enid make us some lemonade or maybe there are some cookies around."

McCall shook her head. Was her grandmother actually nervous? "Why don't you just tell me why you wanted to see me."

"Must you always be so outspoken?" Pepper demanded, then shook her head. "You remind me of myself."

Clearly that was not a good thing.

Her grandmother glanced out the window toward the ridge across the ravine. It was lit with bright sunlight. McCall wondered how many times her grandmother had looked over there thinking about Trace, thinking that he'd been just across that narrow deep expanse all these years.

"I want you to return to the sheriff's department."

McCall blinked, surprised at her grandmother's words as much as her tone. "I beg your pardon?"

"You're too good at your job to quit."

McCall didn't know what to say.

"I think you should run for the sheriff position," Pepper continued.

"Sheriff? I'm afraid a woman deputy is as unorthodox as Whitehorse gets."

"You might be surprised what is possible when you're a Winchester."

McCall laughed. "Quite frankly, having the Winchester name hasn't really been an asset."

Pepper actually looked ashamed. "You and your mother have been treated badly and I'm sorry for that."

McCall stared at her, betting the farm that apologizing wasn't something Pepper Winchester often did.

"I can understand if you say no, but I'd like to make the offer," her grandmother said. "I would be honored if you would have your wedding here at the ranch and, if you'd not be offended, I'd like to pay for it."

McCall was speechless for a moment. "That really isn't—"

"Necessary. I know. It's so little so late."

As McCall looked into her grandmother's dark eyes, so like her own, she willed herself to be careful before trusting her grandmother.

Still, when Pepper said the words, McCall couldn't help the tears that rushed to her eyes or the sudden swell of her heart.

"I think your father would approve. After all, you are Trace's daughter, my granddaughter and a Winchester."

McCall finally felt as if that were true.

PEPPER'S ATTORNEY SOUNDED shocked to hear her voice, probably because it had been twenty-seven years since she'd called him.

"Mrs. Winchester."

"Yes, Curtis, I'm still alive," she said drily, though her lawyer sounded as if he had one foot in the grave. He'd retired years ago, turning his practice over to his nephew.

"I need you to do something for me. Not your nephew."

"Of course." He sounded resigned to whatever it was she wanted.

"Find my family. I want to see them."

He made a surprised sound. "That's wonderful, Pepper. Mending ties with your family is so important at this age. I know you won't be sorry."

She was already sorry and said as much.

"I want you to contact each of them—use your letterhead," Pepper told the attorney. "I've written down what I want you to say on my behalf. Enid will deliver it tomorrow. Do you think you can handle that?"

"I would think this means you are writing a new will."

"Don't think, Curtis. Just do what I ask and make sure no one finds out the terms of my will until I'm gone."

"Of course everything in your will is confidential. You and I are the only two people who know the terms."

"Make sure it stays that way. You will let me know when you have the addresses and the letter ready to mail." She hung up before he could offer any further pleasantries and reread the letter her lawyer would be mailing out.

She nodded to herself, pleased. It would bring her grandchildren back to the ranch. Of course it could also bring the others. She would deal with that when she had to.

What would all of them be like now? Either greedy or curious, she hoped, since the letter would lead them all to believe she was dying and about to divide up her fortune—but only to those who returned to the ranch as she requested.

That, she assured herself, would lure them all back to the Winchester Ranch where she would be waiting for them.

As she looked toward the rocky ridge in the distance, Pepper Winchester knew it was no coincidence that her son had been murdered in sight of the Winchester ranch.

Just as it was no coincidence that a pair of binoculars had been hidden in the third floor room.

As she watched the sun set over the Montana prairie, she swore on her son's grave that once all her family was back on the ranch, she would find out who under this roof twenty-seven years ago had betrayed him. Then there would be hell to pay.

* * * * *

*Harlequin Intrigue top author Delores Fossen
presents a brand-new series
of breathtaking romantic suspense!*
TEXAS MATERNITY: HOSTAGES
*The first installment available May 2010:
THE BABY'S GUARDIAN*

Shaw cursed and hooked his arm around Sabrina.

Despite the urgency that the deadly gunfire created, he tried to be careful with her, and he took the brunt of the fall when he pulled her to the ground. His shoulder hit hard, but he held on tight to his gun so that it wouldn't be jarred from his hand.

Shaw didn't stop there. He crawled over Sabrina, sheltering her pregnant belly with his body, and he came up ready to return fire.

This was obviously a situation he'd wanted to avoid at all cost. He didn't want his baby in the middle of a fight with these armed fugitives, but when they fired that shot, they'd left him no choice. Now, the trick was to get Sabrina safely out of there.

"Get down," someone on the SWAT team yelled from the roof of the adjacent building.

Shaw did. He dropped lower, covering Sabrina as best he could.

There was another shot, but this one came from a rifleman on the SWAT team. Shaw didn't look up, but he heard the sound of glass being blown apart.

The shots continued, all coming from his men, which

meant it might be time to try to get Sabrina to better cover. Shaw glanced at the front of the building.

So that Sabrina's pregnant belly wouldn't be smashed against the ground, Shaw eased off her and moved her to a sitting position so that her back was against the brick wall. They were close. Too close. And face-to-face.

He found himself staring right into those sea-green eyes.

How will Shaw get Sabrina out?
Follow the daring rescue and the heartbreaking
aftermath in THE BABY'S GUARDIAN
by Delores Fossen,
available May 2010 from Harlequin Intrigue.

Copyright © 2010 by Delores Fossen

INTRIGUE

BESTSELLING
HARLEQUIN INTRIGUE® AUTHOR

DELORES
FOSSEN

PRESENTS AN ALL-NEW
THRILLING TRILOGY

TEXAS MATERNITY:
HOSTAGES

When masked gunmen take over the maternity ward
at a San Antonio hospital, local cops, FBI and the scared
mothers can't figure out any possible motive. Before
long, secrets are revealed, and a city that has been on
edge since the siege began learns the truth behind the
negotiations and must deal with the fallout.

LOOK FOR

THE BABY'S GUARDIAN, *May*
DEVASTATING DADDY, *June*
THE MOMMY MYSTERY, *July*

www.eHarlequin.com

HI69472

HARLEQUIN® *Blaze*™

is proud to present

New York Times **bestselling author**

Vicki Lewis Thompson

with a brand-new trilogy,
SONS OF CHANCE
where three sexy brothers
meet three irresistible women.

Look for the first book

WANTED!

Available beginning in June 2010
wherever books are sold.

red-hot reads

www.eHarlequin.com

HB79548

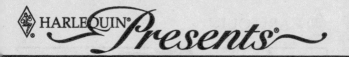

HARLEQUIN *Presents*

Bestselling Harlequin Presents® author

Lynne Graham

introduces

VIRGIN ON HER WEDDING NIGHT

Valente Lorenzatto never forgave Caroline Hales's
abandonment of him at the altar. But now he's
made millions and claimed his aristocratic Venetian
birthright—and he's poised to get his revenge.
He'll ruin Caroline's family by buying out their
company and throwing them out of their mansion...
unless she agrees to give him the wedding night
she denied him five years ago....

**Available May 2010
from Harlequin Presents!**

www.eHarlequin.com

HP12915

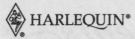 HARLEQUIN®

American ★ *Romance*®

LAURA MARIE ALTOM

The Baby Twins

Stephanie Olmstead has her hands full raising
her twin baby girls on her own. When she runs
into old friend Brady Flynn, she's shocked to find
herself suddenly attracted to the handsome airline
pilot! Will this flyboy be the perfect daddy—
or will he crash and burn?

Babies
&
Bachelors
USA

"LOVE, HOME & HAPPINESS"

www.eHarlequin.com

HAR75309

Love Inspired®

Former bad boy Sloan Hawkins is back in
Redemption, Oklahoma, to help keep his aunt's
cherished garden thriving and to reconnect with the
girl he left behind, Annie Markham. But when he
discovers his secret child—and that single mother
Annie never stopped loving him—he's determined
that a wedding will take place in the garden
nurtured by faith and love.

REDEMPTION
RIVER

Where healing flows...

Look for

The Wedding Garden
by Linda Goodnight

*Available May 2010
wherever you buy books.*

www.SteepleHill.com

Steeple
Hill®

LI87595

LARGER-PRINT BOOKS!

GET 2 FREE LARGER-PRINT NOVELS

HARLEQUIN®
INTRIGUE®

PLUS 2 FREE GIFTS!

Breathtaking Romantic Suspense

YES! Please send me 2 FREE LARGER-PRINT Harlequin Intrigue® novels and my 2 FREE gifts (gifts are worth about $10). After receiving them, if I don't wish to receive any more books, I can return the shipping statement marked "cancel." If I don't cancel, I will receive 6 brand-new novels every month and be billed just $4.99 per book in the U.S. or $5.74 per book in Canada. That's a saving of at least 13% off the cover price! It's quite a bargain! Shipping and handling is just 50¢ per book.* I understand that accepting the 2 free books and gifts places me under no obligation to buy anything. I can always return a shipment and cancel at any time. Even if I never buy another book from Harlequin, the two free books and gifts are mine to keep forever.

199/399 HDN E5MS

Name	(PLEASE PRINT)

Address	Apt. #

City	State/Prov.	Zip/Postal Code

Signature (if under 18, a parent or guardian must sign)

Mail to the Harlequin Reader Service:
IN U.S.A.: P.O. Box 1867, Buffalo, NY 14240-1867
IN CANADA: P.O. Box 609, Fort Erie, Ontario L2A 5X3

Not valid for current subscribers to Harlequin Intrigue Larger-Print books.

Are you a subscriber to Harlequin Intrigue books and want to receive the larger-print edition? Call 1-800-873-8635 today!

* Terms and prices subject to change without notice. Prices do not include applicable taxes. N.Y. residents add applicable sales tax. Canadian residents will be charged applicable provincial taxes and GST. Offer not valid in Quebec. This offer is limited to one order per household. All orders subject to approval. Credit or debit balances in a customer's account(s) may be offset by any other outstanding balance owed by or to the customer. Please allow 4 to 6 weeks for delivery. Offer available while quantities last.

Your Privacy: Harlequin Books is committed to protecting your privacy. Our Privacy Policy is available online at www.eHarlequin.com or upon request from the Reader Service. From time to time we make our lists of customers available to reputable third parties who may have a product or service of interest to you. If you would prefer we not share your name and address, please check here. ☐

Help us get it right—We strive for accurate, respectful and relevant communications. To clarify or modify your communication preferences, visit us at www.ReaderService.com/consumerchoice.

HILP10R

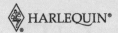

HARLEQUIN®

Showcase

On sale May 11, 2010

Reader favorites from the most talented voices in romance

Save $1.00 on the purchase of 1 or more Harlequin® Showcase books.

SAVE $1.00 on the purchase of 1 or more Harlequin® Showcase books.

Coupon expires Oct 31, 2010. Redeemable at participating retail outlets. Limit one coupon per purchase. Valid in the U.S.A. and Canada only.

52609015

5 65373 00076 2 (8100)0 11651

Canadian Retailers: Harlequin Enterprises Limited will pay the face value of this coupon plus 10.25¢ if submitted by customer for this product only. Any other use constitutes fraud. Coupon is nonassignable. Void if taxed, prohibited or restricted by law. Consumer must pay any government taxes. Void if copied. Nielsen Clearing House ("NCH") customers submit coupons and proof of sales to Harlequin Enterprises Limited, P.O. Box 3000, Saint John, NB E2L 4L3, Canada. Non-NCH retailer—for reimbursement submit coupons and proof of sales directly to Harlequin Enterprises Limited, Retail Marketing Department, 225 Duncan Mill Rd., Don Mills, ON M3B 3K9, Canada.

U.S. Retailers: Harlequin Enterprises Limited will pay the face value of this coupon plus 8¢ if submitted by customer for this product only. Any other use constitutes fraud. Coupon is nonassignable. Void if taxed, prohibited or restricted by law. Consumer must pay any government taxes. Void if copied. For reimbursement submit coupons and proof of sales directly to Harlequin Enterprises Limited, P.O. Box 880478, El Paso, TX 88588-0478, U.S.A. Cash value 1/100 cents.

® and TM are trademarks owned and used by the trademark owner and/or its licensee.
© 2009 Harlequin Enterprises Limited

HSCCOUP0410

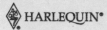

HARLEQUIN®

INTRIGUE®

COMING NEXT MONTH

Available May 11, 2010

#1203 HER BODYGUARD
Bodyguard of the Month
Mallory Kane

#1204 HITCHED!
Whitehorse, Montana: Winchester Ranch
B.J. Daniels

#1205 THE BABY'S GUARDIAN
Texas Maternity: Hostages
Delores Fossen

#1206 STRANDED WITH THE PRINCE
Defending the Crown
Dana Marton

#1207 STRANGER IN A SMALL TOWN
Shivers
Kerry Connor

#1208 MAN UNDERCOVER
Thriller
Alana Matthews

HICNMBPA0410